ACE G·MAN

THE SUICIDE SQUAD
IN CORPSE-TOWN
AND OTHER STORIES

By Emile C. Tepperman

POPULAR PUBLICATIONS • 2022

PUBLISHING HISTORY

"The Suicide Squad in Corpse-Town" originally appeared in the January 1941 (Vol. 8, No. 1) issue of *Ace G-Man Stories* magazine. "The Coffin Barricade" originally appeared in the March 1941 (Vol. 8, No. 2) issue of *Ace G-Man Stories* magazine. "The Tunnel Death Built" originally appeared in the May 1941 (Vol. 8, No. 3) issue of *Ace G-Man Stories* magazine. Copyright 2022 by Argosy Communications, Inc. All rights reserved.

THE SUICIDE SQUAD
IN CORPSE-TOWN

CHAPTER 1
TOWN WITHOUT LAW

S TEPHEN KLAW'S train was on time at Coast City. He made his way off the platform into the station, slightly ahead of the other passengers on the Boston train. The first thing he noticed was the trim, petite figure of Martha Manning, standing by the Information Desk. He recognized her at once by the description they had given him—five-feet-three, about a hundred and two pounds, black hair and eyes, wearing a small green hat and a green sports coat.

She had her eyes anxiously fixed on the main gate, and her gaze followed Steve for a moment as he emerged into the station. But her glance flicked away at once, dismissing him without hesitation. She was not to blame for that. She didn't have a description of him. And furthermore, Stephen Klaw was so slim and wiry that he might have been taken for just another college kid returning to Coast University after the summer vacation. She swung around to watch the gate for the other passengers.

Steve didn't go over to her. Instead, he went first to the bulletin board where the incoming trains were posted, and noted that the five o'clock train from Washington was fourteen minutes

2

late, and would arrive at 7:20. The station clock showed it to be 7:12 now.

He crossed over to the open lunch counter at the other end of the station, and ordered a cup of black coffee. While he drank, he kept his eyes on the mirror behind the counter, in which he could see everything that went on in the station. Martha Manning was getting manifestly more and more nervous as all the passengers from the Boston train departed, and none of them approached her. Steve noted that there were at least two men near the information booth who seemed to be deeply interested in her movements. They were big, heavy-set fellows with a look of complete ruthlessness about them. One, who was studying a travel folder at the counter, not three feet from Martha Manning, had a decided bulge over his right hip pocket. He was wearing a tan reversible raincoat, and he had it open so that there was nothing to impede the movement of his hand toward that pocket. The other man had a gray topcoat. He was strolling around and around the information booth, passing close to Martha Manning each time he came to her side of the booth.

Steve's eyes were expressionless as he noted all this. He sipped his black coffee slowly, while the minute-hand of the clock moved around to 7:20. The Washington train pulled in, and passengers began to trickle out. Steve made no move to get up. In the mirror he spotted the powerful, stevedore shoulders of Johnny Kerrigan and the slender, panther-like figure of Dan Murdoch. His eyes flickered, but he did not turn around. He ordered a second cup of coffee, and waited. A couple of moments later he saw Murdoch and Kerrigan coming up behind him, heard Dan say in a loud voice, "Here, let's grab a cup of Java!"

As if by accident, they ranged themselves alongside of Steve at the counter, and gave their orders. Then, out of the corner of his mouth, Dan Murdoch said, "Hiya, Shrimp?"

Steve covered his lips with the paper napkin. "Okay, Mope. The girl is here—that one in the green coat by the Information Desk. She's being shadowed, so I guess the fun will commence at once."

"Suits me!" Johnny Kerrigan growled. "Let's get started!"

"Right!" said Steve Klaw. "Cover me, but remember—don't interfere unless it's absolutely necessary. If you lose me, look for me in an hour, in front of police headquarters."

He dropped a dime on the counter, and strolled away. He didn't make directly for the Information Desk, but ambled around the station first, looking at the displays in the various shop windows that lined the waiting room. At last he turned in the direction of Martha Manning.

SHE WAS really quite nervous by this time—so nervous that she almost jumped when Steve came up behind her and said. "Miss Manning, I believe?"

Her eyes were blank for a moment as she turned to face him. "Yes," the said. "I'm Miss Manning."

"Name of Klaw," Steve said, grinning, and took a card from his pocket, which he handed to her. She didn't notice that the ink on the card had a fresh, wet look, as if it had only recently been printed.

The card read:

S. KLAW

Attorney & Counselor at Law

"Oh!" she said, fingering the card hesitantly. "You—you're the lawyer my Cousin Jim sent. I thought you weren't coming. I saw you come off the train, but I didn't think you were the one. I—I was looking for a *big* man."

Steve grinned again. "Give me time, Miss Manning. I may grow yet."

She said swiftly, looking up at him, "Oh, forgive me. I—I didn't mean that you're very short." Her eyes appraised him. "You're about five-foot-seven. But—but Jim led me to believe that he was sending a—a fighting man, a lawyer who couldn't be scared easily. You—you look so young—"

"Suppose we forget about that," Steve said crisply. "Let's talk about you. What was it you wanted?"

"Did—did Jim tell you anything?"

"Only that your brother is in trouble, and that you couldn't get a local lawyer to take care of him."

"That's right. My brother Fred is the manager of the Manning Aircraft Corporation, just outside of town. The factory has been closed for three months, while they tooled-up for a new model interceptor plane, for the Royal Air Force."

"I know," said Steve. "I saw something about it in the papers a few months ago. Manning Aircraft is to turn out three hundred of their new M-10 Interceptors, capable of power-diving at six hundred miles an hour. I thought they'd be in production by this time."

"They would have been," Martha Manning said, "except for

one thing—the factory has been condemned by the Coast City Administration!"

"Condemned!" Steve exclaimed. "On what grounds?"

"They're going to use the land for a new park!"

"Have they the right to do that? After all, those planes are for national defense."

"The planes are for England," she told him. "Federal laws don't cover that."

"I see," he said thoughtfully. "So the city has the right to appropriate the factory, tear it down and build a park—as long as they pay the Manning Aircraft Corporation the value of the property."

"Exactly. But it would mean a loss of almost a million dollars to Manning Aircraft. Fred was fighting them tooth and nail in the courts. Last week, he told me he had found evidence which would force Yancey Jervis to give up the idea of condemning the property. He told me he had the evidence safely hidden, and that he was going to have a showdown with Jervis the next day. Jervis controls the political machine here in Coast City, and though he holds no elected office, everybody goes to see him when they want anything done."

"Did your brother see Jervis?"

"No. He was arrested that evening!"

"Arrested?"

"Yes. They've held him without bail on some trumped-up charge, and I can't even find out where he's being held." She paused, breathing hard, then burst out, "And not a lawyer in town will take the case!"

"They afraid of Jervis?"

She nodded. "Jervis can break anybody in this town that he wants to. Nobody dares oppose him."

"I see," Steve said reflectively. "And you want *me* to take the case?"

Her eyes were wide. "I—I don't know what to say, now. You look so young—I'm afraid to think of what they'll do to you—"

"Don't worry about that, Miss Manning," Steve said softly. "I am very happy to accept the case!"

"You're not afraid—"

He shrugged. "Afraid? Sure I am. But—"

"If you're afraid, pal," a hard, crisp voice said behind him, "then you better scram out of town on the next train!"

At the same time, a set of thick, powerful fingers wrapped themselves around his right arm, with a punishing, vise-like grip.

Slowly, Steve turned around.

IT WAS the man in the reversible raincoat. He towered above Steve like a giant, looking down at him out of narrowed, calculating eyes. His thick lips quirked in a twisted, sardonic smile. "I'm Sergeant Keppler, of the Downtown Squad, mister. This—" he jerked his head toward the other man, in the gray topcoat— "is Detective Hassett. We're telling you, mister, that no out-of-town shyster lawyers are wanted here. We're taking you right over to the ticket office, and you can buy yourself a ticket back to Boston—"

Twin points of fire flickered in Stephen Klaw's eyes. He glanced down at the thick, beefy fingers which gripped his arm, then up at Keppler.

"Take your hand off me!" he said softly, almost in a whisper.

Keppler's face flushed. "Don't get tough, punk—"

That was all he said, for Stephen Klaw suddenly went into action. He twisted sharply to the right, dragging Keppler forward. At the same time, his left fist came around in a blindingly swift arc, landing with a thud just behind the big man's right ear.

Keppler grunted, and staggered to one side with the force of the blow, releasing his hold on Klaw's arm. He fell forward, putting out both hands, and rested for an instant pushing down against the floor. Then his elbows buckled, and he went down, flat on his face.

No one, looking at Stephen Klaw's slim and wiry figure, would have deemed him capable of delivering such a powerful blow. But many a man had been deceived in the past by outward appearances. And no one had ever tangled with Stephen Klaw once, without watching his step in the future.

Steve heard a gasp from Martha Manning, and swung around in time to see the other man, Detective Hassett, coming at him. Hassett's face was twisted with rage, and he was clawing a blackjack out of his pocket.

Steve grinned thinly and set himself to meet the attack. But just then the big bulk of Johnny Kerrigan interposed itself between him and Hassett. Johnny's shoulder as if accidentally, jolted into Hassett's jaw, and then Johnny grabbed the big detective by the arm.

"Why, if it isn't my old friend. Joe Doke!" he shouted, slapping

Hassett so hard on the back that the man almost doubled over. "How've you been all these years, Joe?"

Hassett almost spat with rage. "Get out of the way, you thick lug. My name ain't Joe Doke—"

Johnny winked at Steve, and slapped him again, harder.

"Sure you're Joe Doke. You can't fool me! Come on, I'll buy you a drink—"

Steve saw that a small crowd was gathering. Dan Murdoch was bending over the prone figure of Sergeant Keppler, and he was yelling, "Give him air! It's a heart attack!"

Steve winked back at Johnny, turned swiftly and took Martha Manning's arm.

"Let's get out of here!" he said, and led her away. None of the crowd had seen the inception of the brawl, and they didn't connect Steve and Martha with it at all. As they reached the street door, Steve heard Hassett shouting, "Damn you, you're obstructing the law—"

HE TURNED and saw that Johnny had a bear grip on the detective's arm, and was acting as if he were intoxicated, while Dan Murdoch was helping Keppler to his feet. He grinned, and pushed Martha Manning out into the street, and got her into a taxicab at the curb.

"Downtown!" he ordered.

The cab got going, and the driver asked over his shoulder, "Whereabouts downtown, mister?"

"Just keep driving," Steve told him. "I'll let you know later."

He turned and looked at Martha Manning, who was watching him, puzzled.

"I—I don't understand what happened," she gasped. "I thought those men were going to run you out of town, and then you had hit the one, and the big blond man took care of the other. Who—who is that big blond man?"

Steve grinned. "He's my interference. He and the dark, handsome lad. The three of us always work together. Their names are Kerrigan and Murdoch."

For a moment there was a vague look in her eyes, and then she gasped. "Kerrigan and Murdoch. And you're Klaw! Of course I've heard of you. Kerrigan and Murdoch and Klaw— the Suicide Squad. You—you're not a lawyer. You're G-men—"

"We're lawyers, too," Steve told her gravely. "Sometimes people forget that. A good many G-men are lawyers."

"But how did Jim come to send you—"

"The F.B.I. has been trying to get Jervis for a long time," Stephen Klaw told her. "Your cousin, Jim Raynor, knew that. So when he got your call, he contacted the Chief of the F.B.I., and made arrangements for me to come here."

"Oh!" There was suddenly a glad light in her eyes. "Then there's a chance for Fred? You'll help me get him free?"

"I'll do the best I can, Martha Manning. Just give me a lead of some kind. Who would know where they're holding your brother?"

Her shoulders sagged. "I've been everywhere—to the District Attorney, the Police Commissioner, even to Boss Jervis, himself!"

"And what did Jervis say?" Steve demanded tightly.

"He's too smooth to commit himself. But he gave me to understand that if I knew where Fred has hidden the evidence he gathered, I should turn it over to him, and then he would use his influence to have Fred released."

"Do you know where the evidence is hidden?"

"No. If I knew where it is, I'd give it up—because I think he'll—kill my brother otherwise!"

Steve laughed shortly. "Killing isn't so easy to get away with."

She waved her hand impatiently. "No, no, you don't understand. Jervis has a strangle-hold on the police department, on the District Attorney's office, and on almost every official department of the city. They obey him like a dictator. It would be easy for them to cook up a story that Fred was shot while attempting to escape. Jervis practically hinted as much to me."

"Ah!" said Stephen Klaw. "This begins to interest me!"

He leaned forward and pushed open the pane of glass which separated them from the driver's seat. "Take us down to police headquarters!" he ordered crisply, and slid the pane shut again.

Martha Manning stared at him, wide-eyed.

"That's suicide!" she gasped. "They'll—arrest you on some pretext, and beat the life out of you. That's why no lawyer in town would accept my case. Several attorneys who tried to buck Jervis hare landed in the hospital—"

"Maybe they won't have such an easy job with this attorney!" Steve said softly.

CHAPTER 2
ONE VULNERABLE ALLY

A S T H E cab threaded its way downtown, they saw several police cars dashing by, with sirens wide open, screaming signals blasting deafeningly against their eardrums. One of the cars sped north as they rode south, and their driver narrowly avoided a head-on collision. A little farther down, another squad car skittered around a corner on two wheels, and also headed north toward the station.

Martha Manning grew tense as she sat beside Stephen Klaw. "I wonder what's happened—"

Steve reached up and switched on the radio. In a moment they got an announcer's voice: *"Coast City Police have broadcast an alarm for two thugs who viciously attacked a Detective Sergeant and a First Grade Detective in the Grand Concourse of Central Station a few minutes ago. The thugs surprised the two detectives, slugging them from behind, with no apparent motive. Then, taking the guns of the stricken detectives, they made good their escape through the railroad station. Though the identity of these thugs is as yet unknown, their quick capture is considered certain...."*

"Good Lord!" Martha Manning gasped. "Those are your two partners—Kerrigan and Murdoch. They'll be shot down like dogs!"

Stephen Klaw chuckled, and shut off the radio.

"Don't worry about those two lads," he told her. "They know how to take care of themselves. They'll be right on deck when they're needed!"

Martha's lower lip was trembling just a little, with the faint hint of a hesitant smile. "I'm beginning to hope again," she whispered. "To hope that Fred may be saved!"

Steve wasn't listening to her. He was thinking. Suddenly he snapped his fingers. He leaned forward again, and slid the front pane open.

"Stop at the nearest phone!" he ordered.

The driver pulled in to the curb at the next corner, in front of a drug store.

"Wait here," Steve said, and pushed out of the cab. He entered the drug store, and slipped into a telephone booth. He took from his pocket a small typewritten sheet which had been furnished to him in Boston. It contained the private telephone numbers of some fifteen officials of Coast City. None of these numbers were listed in the phone book, but it had been easy for the F.B.I. to compile them.

Klaw dialed one of those numbers, and waited till he got the connection. Then he said, "Please let me talk with Mr. Yancey Jervis. It is on a matter of the utmost importance to him."

A voice at the other end asked cautiously, "Who's this calling, please?"

"Never mind who this is!" Steve snapped. "Put Jervis on—quick!"

There was a moment's pause, and then another voice said, "This is Jervis speaking. What can I do for you?"

"Hello, Mr. Jervis," Steve said, thickening his own voice just a bit. "I'm phoning to give you a tip—better release Fred

Manning—pronto. There'll be hell popping if he isn't out in twenty minutes."

"Who are you?" Jervis demanded sharply.

"THIS IS one of the guys that smacked your stooge detectives around, over at the railroad station a while ago. When Keppler and Hassett wake up, they'll tell you it isn't healthy to fool around with us. So take a tip—release Fred Manning!"

"I see," Yancey Jervis said slowly. "Now let me get this straight. You boys have come to town for the purpose of effecting Fred Manning's release—is that it?"

"That's one of our purposes," Steve said.

"And what are the others, if I may ask?"

Steve grinned. "We'll let you know in due time, Jervis. We like to work on one thing at a time. Right now, it's Fred Manning."

"I see. And you are the men whom the police are hunting in the vicinity of the railroad station?"

"That's right, Jervis. Only we aren't at the station any more. Now what do you say—do you release Fred Manning, or do we bear down on you?"

"Hold the wire a moment, please. The District Attorney—Mr. Clarence Bell—happens to be right here with me. I'll ask him what can be done. Hold on now—"

"Sure," said Steve. He grinned faintly and gently put the receiver down on the shelf alongside the phone, without hanging up. Then he stepped out of the booth and hurried swiftly back to the waiting taxicab.

Martha Manning watched him tensely as he climbed in.

"Okay," he said to the driver. "Straight for Police Headquarters now!"

As they turned the next corner, a police radio car streamed to a stop in front of the drug store they had just left. Also, the sound of another radio car siren cut through the air from the north.

Steve nodded in satisfaction, and winked at Martha.

"They're coming back," he said.

She asked breathlessly, "What—what did you do in there?"

"I called off the dogs from the Central Station. In five minutes, every police car up there, will be converging on that drug store. That'll relieve the pressure on Kerrigan and Murdoch, and give them a chance to make good their escape!"

Martha smiled happily, showing a dimple in each cheek.

"The Suicide Squad!" she said dreamily. "I've read about you, in magazine articles. They say you three are madmen, the way you take wild and unbelievable risks. But—I'm beginning to think there's method in your madness!"

"Thank you," Stephen Klaw said modestly. He turned on the radio again, but there was no more news. Five minutes more of steady driving through traffic, and they came in sight of police headquarters.

"Pull over and park across the street from headquarters," Steve ordered the cabby. "We're waiting for some one."

With the cab parked, Klaw turned on the radio once more.

"...on a tip from an influential citizen, the police sped, a few minutes ago, to a drug store on the East Side, in search of the two narcotic-maddened thugs who are terrorizing the city. One of these thugs had the audacity to telephone to the Honorable Yancey Jervis," *demanding a huge sum as the price of safety. They threatened to kill Mr. Jervis if he did not pay over the money by midnight. Mr. Jervis, exercising great presence of mind, signalled his secretary to call police headquarters on another phone, while he endeavored to hold the gunman in conversation. The call was traced, but unfortunately, Mr. Jervis's ruse did not succeed. The gunmen had already fled. Police Commissioner Gilz states that their capture is only a matter of hours...."*

Stephen Klaw laughed harshly.

"Jervis has a good imagination," he said. "He invented that ransom story out of whole cloth."

"You didn't demand ransom?" Martha asked.

"No. All I asked was that he release your brother. He couldn't very well make *that* public, so he made up the ransom story."

MARTHA MANNING shuddered. "I hate to think at what the police will do to your two friends if they catch them—and to you, too, for that matter. Commissioner Gilz used to be a labor spy racketeer. He was made Commissioner by Yancey Jervis, and then he brought in a small army of his hoodlums, and made then police officers and detectives. Now they're running the whole city as if it were their own private racket!"

Steve nodded, his lips tightly compressed. "We know all that. The Department of Justice has been watching Coast City for a long time. We know just how rotten it is—"

"And you haven't done anything about it?" she exclaimed. "You haven't tried to stop it—"

"Stop it? How could we? The F.B.I. has jurisdiction in federal offenses, but not in local matters. Kerrigan and Murdoch and I

17

have no legal right to be here. We're acting as private citizens, not as Special Agents of the Federal Bureau of Investigation."

"Then why—why did you come at all? Surely not for my sake—"

"No, not for your sake alone, Martha Manning." Stephen Klaw hesitated, studying her with keen eyes, appraising her firm, youthful beauty, and the honest, candid way in which she met his glance.

"I'm going to trust you with a secret, Martha," he went on slowly. "Kerrigan and Murdoch and I would have come here anyway. There's something bigger in the fire than even your brother's life."

"Something bigger? I don't understand."

Steve Klaw lowered his voice. "The F.B.I. was going to start an investigation of Yancey Jervis's income-tax reports. We had enough information already, to indicate that it would be easy to indict him. And suddenly, yesterday, our Chief got a call from one of the key Senators in the United States Senate, the chairman of an important committee. That Senator literally begged the Chief to drop the investigation for the time being. He even offered to resign from the Senate if the Chief would lay off. He wouldn't give any reason for the request, but swore that it was a matter of life and death."

Martha's eyes were wide, open. "A senator! Which one?"

Steve smiled, and shook his head. "Let's call him Senator Blank. The Chief promised Senator Blank that he would drop the official investigation for the time being. But he sent Kerrigan and Murdoch and myself here to Coast City, to find out what was behind it. It just happened that your cousin contacted us about your call, and we decided we'd use your brother's trouble as a cloak for our own operations."

For a moment. Martha Manning was silent. Then she said bitterly, "Thanks for being so frank. Mr. Klaw. So all the hope I was beginning to feel was just a day-dream! You're not going to help me at all—"

"On the contrary, Martha Manning," Steve said softly, "I'm going to help you get your brother free. I promise that I'll do everything in my power to help you—on one condition."

"Yes?"

"That *you* help *me.*"

"Of course I will!" she said eagerly. "I'll help. I'll do *anything* you ask of me."

"It may be dangerous—"

"I don't care!"

"It's a bargain, then!"

SHE THRUST out her hand like a man, and they shook. There was a hint of moisture in her eyes. "I—thought for a moment, when you told me about the other thing—that you were only using me as a tool, for your own ends. But now—I'm glad you've told me. I—begin to understand how you three men work!"

Steve grinned and pointed across the street. "*There's* an example of how we work!"

She followed his glance and frowned, looking at the small paneled truck which had pulled up in front of the Headquarters Building.

"I don't understand. That's just a Water Inspector's car. What has that to do with how you work? All I can see is a Water Inspector and an assistant, getting out. They must be going in to Headquarters to make an inspection—"

Suddenly she gasped, as she got a clear view of the two men who had descended from the Water Inspector's car. They were both attired in Sanitation Department uniforms, but as they turned deliberately and grinned across the street at Steve's cab, their faces were revealed under the visors of the uniform caps. They were the faces of Johnny Kerrigan and Dan Murdoch.

"I can't believe it!" she breathed. "With the whole city hunting them—they turn up here! And how could they have gotten the car and the uniforms—"

Steve chuckled. "They must have run into the car and its occupants, on one of the side-streets off the station."

"And they took the men's uniforms?"

"Sure. Why not? All's fair in war. The real inspectors are probably trussed up, inside the truck."

He leaned past her, poked his head out the window, and waved to them.

Kerrigan and Murdoch waved back. Dan jerked his thumb toward the entrance of the Headquarters Building, and Steve nodded. Johnny grinned, and took out a leather-bound notebook and pencil. He scribbled something on one of the pages, tore out the page and wadded it into a ball. Then he dropped it at the curb.

Kerrigan and Murdoch then turned and went up the steps of Police Headquarters.

Watching them, Martha Manning uttered a tremorous exclamation of fright.

"They're going inside! They're sticking their heads in the lion's mouth!"

"Sure," said Steve.

"But—but they're hunted men. They'll be shot on sight—"

"Not in Police Headquarters." Steve told her. "Nobody will think of looking for them there?" He took out a slip of paper, and a pencil. "Quick now. Give me your address!"

"Eight-fourteen Silver Street—"

"Phone number?"

"Tiffany 2-3647—"

"Right. Now tell me this—when you tailed your cousin, Jim Raynor, and asked for help, did you phone him from your home?"

"Yes—"

"Then don't use your phone for any important calls. Be careful to say nothing about what I've told you!"

"But why—"

"Don't you see? Your cousin told you over the phone that he was sending you a lawyer, didn't he?"

"Yes."

"Did you mention it to anyone else?"

"No."

"Then why do you think Keppler and Hassett were waiting at the station? How do you think they knew I was the lawyer you were expecting?"

She stared at him with sudden dawning comprehension. "You mean—my wire has been tapped?"

21

"Of course! Jervis is no fool. Now listen to me carefully. "I want you to go home, and wait for me—"

"No, no! I want to stay here. I want to help—"

"There's only one way you can help. By obeying orders. Don't forget that your brother Fred is being held incommunicado somewhere. They're probably torturing him, to make him reveal the hiding place of his evidence. Every minute that you delay me by arguing, may bring your brother a minute closer to death!"

She gulped, and her shoulders straightened. "I'm sorry, Stephen Klaw. I—I was a fool. I'll do whatever you say."

He smiled. "Good. Go home now, and wait till you hear from me. I'll either come, or I'll phone you—"

"But, you just said my wire is tapped—"

"I know. When the phone rings, you'll pick it up and say hello. I'll ask you if this is a certain number. The number I'll mention won't be your number. *It'll be the number of the phone from which I'll be calling!*"

"I see," she whispered, her eyes shining with excitement. "I'd never have thought of a trick like that in a thousand years—"

Steve brushed her remark aside, and hurried on. "You'll say, *wrong number,* and hang up. Then you'll go straight downstairs to a public phone booth, and call the number I mentioned. Do you get it?"

"I get it, Steve. I understand!"

"Okay, Martha. Good luck."

He pressed her hand, then he opened the door of the cab, and stepped out. He gave the driver a ten dollar bill.

"Take the young lady back uptown," he ordered, and started across the street toward the entrance of Police Headquarters.

As the cab started, Martha Manning looked back after his slim and wiry figure. Now her eyes were frankly wet.

"Good luck to *you!*" she whispered.

CHAPTER 3
MURDER WORKS FOR SPIES

AT THE curb in front of Headquarters, Stephen Klaw stooped to tie his shoelace, and picked up the wadded ball of paper which Johnny Kerrigan had dropped there for him. He smoothed it out and read:

> Was it you who got all the cops off our tail, Shrimp? If so—nice work, lad. Watch your step coming inside. You may trip right over us. If the going gets tough, give the old bugle call. See you in hell.

Steve grinned, and tore the paper to bits. He dropped it under the Water Department truck, and went into Police Headquarters without looking behind him. The first thing he saw when he got inside was Johnny Kerrigan and Dan Murdoch, talking with the desk sergeant.

"We're new men on the Water Department," Johnny was saying in a loud, foghorn voice, "an' we says to the chief inspector, 'Why don't you send a couple of the other boys, who know their way around headquarters?' But the chief inspector says, 'Go on down there, you heels, an' check on the water pressure, an' don't argue!' So here we are!"

Johnny spread his hands helplessly. "What can you do with a guy like that?"

"That's what I say!" Dan Murdoch snorted. "We gotta find our way all over the damned building without a blueprint of the water lines—"

"So what do you want me to do about it?" the desk sergeant growled. "It's your headache. Go ahead. The building's yours."

He waved his hand in the direction of the rear. "You'll find all the lines and the meters in the cellar. Now scram, and don't bother me. Don't you see I'm busy?" He flipped his thumb at Stephen Klaw, who had come up to the desk and was standing there quietly, with his hat in his hand.

Johnny Kerrigan turned around and gave Steve a cold stare.

"Huh!" he said, nudging Dan Murdoch. "The guy's a lawyer. I can tell by the way he holds his hat. I bet you he's a lawyer."

"Nuts," said Murdoch, his eyes twinkling. "He looks to me like an insurance salesman. All insurance salesmen are shrimps."

"You're crazy," Johnny protested. "The guy I bought my last policy from was six-foot-two. This guy is a lawyer, I'm a good judge of human stature. Mister—" he appealed to Steve—"are you a lawyer, or ain't you? I'll just be a buck that…."

"My profession," Steve said with frigid dignity, "is that of attorney and counselor-at-law. And now, perhaps you will step out of the way and go about your—er—business, while I speak with the sergeant!"

"Sure, sure," Johnny said, and took Dan by the arm. The two of them disappeared toward the rear of the building.

Half a dozen plain-clothes detectives were lounging around the place, waiting for calls, while a small group of men were listening to a portable radio in a corner. Behind the desk sergeant there was a switch-board with a police officer on duty. None of these men had the appearance of bona-fide law-enforcing officers. Steve was reminded of what Martha had told him—how Commissioner Gilz had imported hoodlums and given them uniforms.

Nothing of what he thought showed in his face as he met the inquiring gaze of the desk sergeant. He took out one of his legal cards, and handed it across the desk.

"I should like to speak with Commissioner Gilz," he said primly. "At once."

The sergeant inspected the card, and frowned.

"S. Klaw. Counselor-at-law," he read. "From Boston, eh? What'd you want to see the Commissioner about?"

"I have been retained," Steve said, "to represent a young man who has been arrested—Frederick Manning!"

THE DESK sergeant almost jumped out of his chair. A startled murmur rose from the men who were lounging around. Suddenly, Steve found that three or four of them had moved in close, so that they formed a semicircle behind him.

Steve put his hat back on his head, and slipped his hands into his coat pockets.

The desk sergeant frowned, and shook his head faintly at the men who had closed in. Then he said to Steve, "You came all the way from Boston to handle Fred Manning's case?"

"That is correct."

"Who hired you?"

"That, my good man, is none of your damned business!"

"*What?*"

"I said that it was none of your damned business!" Steve said firmly. "No one has the right to demand that information of an attorney. You are exceeding your rights, and I shall make it a point to mention the matter to Commissioner Gilz."

"All right, Counselor, you don't have to get mad." The sergeant grinned slyly, and winked at his men. "I was just wondering what time you arrived in Coast City, and whether there was anyone to meet you at the station. I suppose its Manning's sister who hired you."

Steve appeared to consider the matter, and then he shrugged. "It isn't really important. I may as well tell you that I came at the request of Miss Martha Manning. There was some sort of fracas at the station, and I was separated from her, so I came down here alone. And now, if you please, I must insist on seeing Commissioner Gilz."

"Okay, Counselor, okay. I'll take you to him myself!"

The desk sergeant got up and came around in front of the desk, and took Steve by the arm. "This way—"

He led the way almost at a trot, to the stairs, and up to the mezzanine. There were a number of offices here, and he stopped before one of them, on the door of which was lettered only the single word: *Private*.

He knocked twice, and the door was immediately opened by a scrawny man in an alpaca jacket, who was viciously chewing on a toothpick. Steve got a glimpse of the interior of the room. He saw five or six men seated around a desk. Most of them were in police uniform, with gold bars on their shoulders. They would be Captains and Inspectors. Seated at the desk facing those officers was a man with a coarse, thick-featured face, and a pendulous lower lip. Steve recognized that man from pictures in the F.B.I. files, as Grover Gilz, the former labor spy racketeer, and present Police Commissioner of Coast City. This must be a conference which they had interrupted. This was borne out by the man in the alpaca jacket at the door.

"What the hell do you want, Sergeant Wister?" he demanded of Steve's escort.

"Weren't you told the Commissioner was in conference with the department heads?"

"I know, Inspector Simpkin," Wister said. "But this is important. This guy—" nodding at Steve—"is a lawyer named S. Klaw, from Boston."

"So what?" Simpkin demanded, wiggling the toothpick with his lips, and sort of talking around it. "So what?"

Wister looked triumphant. *"He's* the lawyer that Martha Manning hired to defend her brother."

Simpkin took the toothpick out of his mouth, and looked at Steve.

"Well, well!" he said, and stepped to one side. "Come right in, Mr. S. Klaw, of Boston!"

"A pleasure," said Steve, and stepped into the room, with his hands dug deep in his pockets.

Wister came in after him, quickly, and pushed the door shut, locking it behind them.

STEPHEN KLAW moved over to one side, with his back to the wall, and faced the group of police officials, who were all staring at him.

"I must apologize for interrupting your conference, Commissioner, but I owe it to my client to demand that he be arraigned before a judge at once, or else released!"

Commissioner Gilz came slowly to his feet. His face was heavy with anger.

"Counselor," he said, "it's too bad you didn't meet the reception committee I sent down the station to wait for you. But I can tell you what message they had for you. Would you like to hear it?"

Klaw smiled with his lips, but not with his eyes. "No, my dear Commissioner, it will be unnecessary for you to tell me. I know what they were there for. It was their job to see that I bought a return ticket to Boston, and left at once."

"Ah!" said Gilz. "So you know!"

"Yes," Steve told him. "I know. But please note that I'm still in Coast City."

"Meaning what?"

There was suddenly a dead silence in the room as the assembled men watched the slim, youthful looking visitor who had not yet removed his hands from his pockets.

"Meaning what?" Gilz repeated.

"Meaning that it'll take more than you and your whole damned department to run me out of town, Gilz. I'm staying till Manning is released. I want to know where you're holding him, and on what charge."

Gilz studied him for a long, tense minute. Then he said abruptly, "You're no shyster lawyer. I can judge men. You look young, but you're tough. Tough, and Big Time."

He paused a moment, then rested his hands on the desk and leaned forward. *"Just who are you?"*

Steve's eyes were veiled. "Only a lawyer from Boston, Commissioner. Only a lawyer from Boston, who's going to get Fred Manning out of jail—even if I have to pull your town apart to do it!"

Gilz had a puzzled glint in his eyes. He looked around the room at the others, as if asking their opinion.

Inspector Simpkin, who had stood chewing his toothpick and saying nothing, spoke now for the first time.

"I think this guy is from a Boston mob. They may be trying to muscle in. We could fingerprint him, and get the lowdown." He spat out the toothpick, and grinned. "That's where we got the advantage over mobs in other towns. We can use police facilities!"

There was a murmur of assent from the others.

Commissioner Gilz nodded. "A good idea, Simpkin. Grab him, boys, and we'll take his prints. Then we'll throw him in a cell till we get his record. A couple of you boys can work on him in the meanwhile, to sort of tame him, and make him talkative."

The uniformed men sprang up from their chairs and at the same time Simpkin and Wister moved in toward Steve.

Steve didn't attempt to escape. He merely leaned back against the wall, and took his hands our of his pockets. In each of them there was a black, ugly little automatic. He snicked off the safety catches, and held the two guns level, at his hips. He smiled tolerantly at the men who were crowding slowly, menacingly toward him.

"Sure," he said. "Come and get me, boys!"

His hands had slid out of his pockets so smoothly and easily, that they hadn't known what he was doing until they saw the black holes of the guns gaping at their stomachs. Somehow, they hadn't expected anything like that from the slim and youthful looking attorney—in spite of the fact that he had talked so tough. And his seemingly unhurried, almost casual attitude had fooled them.

The rush to seize him stopped short, as if they had come up against an invisible wall. Wister and Simpkin backed away into the others, with their hands well away from their bodies. But those behind began clawing for guns.

Steve's eyes were everywhere at once. He saw those in back reaching for weapons, and he saw Grover Gilz swooping down toward a drawer in his desk.

Steve smiled bleakly and raised his left hand gun. He pointed it over the heads of the men, and fired two shots into the pane of the high window behind Gilz's back.

Almost at once, as if it had been an awaited signal, every light in the room went out.

CHAPTER 4
MESSAGES OF DOOM

T HE SUDDEN blackness which enveloped that room was all the more terrifying because of its unexpectedness. There were gasps of dismay, almost drowned out by the bouncing echoes of Steve's two shots, which were still rolling from wall to wall. Some one shouted. "Cover the door! He's got friends somewhere in the building. They pulled the main switch!"

Steve chuckled soundlessly, and reached over, pawing in the dark for the door. He found the catch, which Wister had locked, and twisted it open. Then he turned the knob swiftly, and yanked the door wide. The mezzanine outside was in pitch darkness, as was the rest of the building. From somewhere out in the main foyer, a man's voice sounded, cursing methodically.

Within the room, as Steve hugged the wall, there was a rush of feet toward the door. No one of those uniformed officials dared to switch on a flashlight, for they had seen the guns in Klaw's hands, and they had no wish to draw his fire. But from the direction of the desk came Grover Gilz's thick, angry voice: *"The door, you fools! He's making his getaway!"*

Most of the uniformed officials were already through the door, feeling their way out into the hall. The others followed.

Steve was already most of the way around the room, following the wall. Gilz foolishly revealed his exact position by bawling further orders in the dark. Steve followed his voice as if it were a radio beam, with his guns thrust out before him. He felt the muzzle of his left-hand gun suddenly poke into a yielding

31

body, and Gilz's angry voice was transformed into a frightened gasp. The man recoiled in the dark, and Steve came in after him swiftly, slapping at where he guessed his head to be with the muzzle of his right-hand gun. He felt the end of the barrel graze against bone, and there was a grunt, then a crash as Gilz tumbled over his own chair.

Steve dropped one of the guns in his pocket, and brought out a small flashlight. He flicked it on, turned the beam down upon the unconscious form of the Police Commissioner, huddled on the floor, tangled up with the chair.

Out in the hall, men were shouting, cursing, swearing. Many of them had now produced flashlights, and the mezzanine out there was criss-crossed with stabbing beams of light. Steve sprang over to the door, pushed it shut, and turned the catch. Some one in the hall shouted, "Hey! He's in the Commissioner's office! He's locked the door!"

There was a tumultuous rush of feet outside, and men's bodies crashed against the door. But it did not give.

Stephen Klaw paid no attention to the pounding against the door. He hurried to the window, and leaned out. He saw a pair of headlights swing around the corner from the street in front of the building, saw the Water Inspector's truck moving slowly toward him, with the headlights blinking. Steve grinned, and took out his flashlight. He flicked it on and off three times, and the headlights stopped blinking. The truck veered in sharply, jumped the curb, and pulled up to a halt on the sidewalk, directly beneath his window. Johnny Kerrigan leaned out from behind the wheel and yelled, "Hiya, Shrimp?"

"Okay, Mope," Steve called. "Stand by to receive cargo!"

"Aye, aye, Shrimp!" came Dan Murdoch's voice. Murdoch jumped out from the other side, where he had been sitting beside Johnny, and climbing lithely up onto the roof of the truck. Steve had already stooped down and picked up the inert form of Police Commissioner Gilz. Although Gilz was a heavy man, Steve swung him easily over the window sill. Murdoch's shoulders came level with the sill, and it was simple for him to receive the unconscious Commissioner, and to lower him down to Johnny Kerrigan, who had climbed out from under the wheel.

Stephen Klaw said, "Wait a minute, Dan," and went back to the Commissioner's desk. Men were still smashing at the door, but he didn't even glance in that direction. He went swiftly through each of the drawers in turn, with the aid of his flashlight. In one of the drawers he found a folder marked "Manning." In another drawer he found a long white envelope, on which there was no mark whatever. By the feel of it he could tell what it contained, not papers, but just two keys. He was intrigued by that envelope, and he stuck it in his pocket. There was no time now for further search, for he heard one of the men in the hall shout, "The window! Get around to the outside!"

STEVE TOOK the folder, and climbed out of the window. He stepped out on to the roof of the truck, then vaulted down to the sidewalk.

Johnny Kerrigan had already loaded the unconscious body of Commissioner Gilz into the interior of the truck. He was seated behind the wheel, ready to go. Dan Murdoch slapped Steve on the back, and they both climbed up alongside Johnny.

"Nice work," said Steve. "I think we are through here."

"In that case," Johnny Kerrigan said gravely, "we might as well go away—"

"Fast," said Dan Murdoch.

"Right," said Johnny, and gave her the gas. The truck leaped off the sidewalk and sped down the street under Johnny's expert guidance. In a moment they had rounded the next corner, and were speeding uptown.

"Did you boys check the water pressure down there?" Steve asked.

"We never got to it," Murdoch said ruefully. "Imagine our embarrassment when we ran into the electric light fuses. When you started giving the bugle call with your guns, we had just found the fuse box. There were twenty-eight fuses altogether and it would have taken too long to pull them all out, one at a time, so I just yanked the lead wire out, terminals and all. I'm afraid they won't have any light in headquarters for quite a while!"

Steve was examining the Manning folder, holding it under the dashlight. It contained all the papers in the Manning case, which Gilz had evidently taken from the official flies, and kept secret. Steve looked through them quickly.

"It seems they're holding Fred Manning on a charge of 'Conspiracy,' which doesn't mean a thing. He was committed on a short affidavit, signed by the arresting officer. By using the short affidavit, they don't have to give the details of the crime with which he is charged, until he is arraigned."

"And if nobody makes them arraign him," Dan said, "they can hold him for the rest of his life!"

"It's a nice racket they've got!" Johnny growled. "Does that folder show *where* they're holding him?"

"No," said Steve. "There's nothing—"

He paused, and bent down to examine a penciled telephone number on the cover of the folder. And just as he bent his head, something went *ping,* and then *crunch,* and a hole appeared in the windshield at a spot equidistant between himself and Dan Murdoch. A thousand crinkly little wrinkles appeared in the glass. And almost at once, more *pings* sounded, and more holes blossomed in the windshield. They formed a straight line, coming down toward Steve's head. At the same time, the *rat-tat-tat* of a machine-gun began to crackle from somewhere behind them.

Without taking the time to think about it, Johnny Kerrigan slewed the truck over to the right, stepping down hard on the gas as he did so. The truck leaped ahead like a wounded jackrabbit, and Johnny straightened her out again with the motor roaring.

Stephen Klaw had his gun out, and was leaning far over on his side, peering at the police car which was coming up fast, behind them. A man on the running-board in police uniform had a sub-machine gun at his shoulder, and it was from this weapon that the streamer of bullets was coming. Only the fact that Johnny Kerrigan had veered the truck to suddenly had saved their lives. The police car had been creeping up on them from the left, and Johnny's sudden maneuver had put them behind. The driver of the police car swung his wheel around sharply to regain his same relative position, and that caused the machine-gunner on the running-board to lose his target for the moment. The rest of the burst went wild.

But the gunner, with one arm wrapped around the window-frame of the car, grimly swung his weapon around, sighting it for another burst.

STEPHEN KLAW, hanging far out of the cab of their truck, flipped up his automatic and snapped two quick shots at the front tires of the speeding police car. He hit with both bullets, but nothing happened. The police car continued on its rocket-like course in their wake. Steve frowned. Those tires were solid.

There was only one more thing to do, and he did it. He raised the automatic, sighted carefully at the machine-gunner, and pulled his trigger just a split-instant before the man squeezed the trip of the machine-gun.

Steve's gun barked, flame lanced from the muzzle, and the bullet smashed into the fellow's left shoulder. The man uttered a screech, and let go his hold on the window frame. He toppled backward off the running-board, to land on his back in the road-way, and the machine-gun skittered across the street.

But the police car did not stop. Another man poked his head out of the window, with a riot gun his hands. Steve saw the man rest the riot gun on the windowsill and turn the muzzle directly toward them. The truck was losing to the police car. The distance between them was diminishing; those squad cars were built for speed, and the Water Department truck was not. Steve saw the black muzzle come closer. There was not enough of the gunner's face visible to shoot at, so Steve fired three times, fast, at the windshield. But his slugs flattened themselves against the car's bullet-proof glass.

Now the police car was within range of the riot gun. At this point-blank distance, the steel shot in the charge would smash through the cab of the truck, and riddle all three of them.

"You'll have to crash 'em, Johnny!" Klaw yelled to Kerrigan, and swung back inside the tab.

Johnny Kerrigan nodded grimly, and yanked the wheel hard over to the left, stepping down on the brake at the same time. The truck slewed over to the left and the tires screamed and sizzled. The truck stopped with a shock as if it had hit a brick wall, squarely in the middle of the street, in the path of the oncoming police car.

Kerrigan and Murdoch and Klaw had braced themselves for the impact, but they were nevertheless thrown forward against the windshield by the sudden jolt.

They heard a yell of fright from the police car, and Steve saw the vehicle veer crazily over to the left as the driver made a frantic attempt to avoid hitting them. Steve saw the driver's face for a moment, contorted with fear. Then the police car sped past them. The man had managed to miss them by a breath. But he did not avoid disaster. For he had lost control of the wheel, and the police car mounted the sidewalk, bounced high, twisted in the air, and came down with a crash against the brick wall of a bank building at the corner.

The door jarred open, and men tumbled out. There were four of them, and they all had guns in their hands, but they were dazed and shocked, and they had no desire to use their weapons. They merely stumbled about in a daze, as if they were drunk.

Stephen Klaw turned to Kerrigan. "That was a nice piece of work, Johnny. Don't you think it was a nice piece of work, Mr. Murdoch?"

Dan grinned. "The power of brawn over brains. Now you and I, Mr. Klaw, could never have turned that wheel like that, with just our brains."

"That's right," he said. "With our brains, and Johnny's muscle, we ought to be elected president some day."

"Aw, go to hell!" Johnny grunted, as he stepped on the starter and backed the truck up, then swung it around and headed it down the street.

A crowd was coming on the run, but no one attempted to stop them as they raced out of the block.

JOHNNY DROVE three blocks south, then turned east and parked in a dark factory street over near the river. He turned off the ignition, and wiped sweat from his forehead.

"Well," he grinned, "I guess we can't use our pretty Water Department truck any more."

Steve shook his head. "I guess not. Too bad there's no radio in here. They must have broadcast an alarm for us at once. Every prowl car in the city will be on the lookout for this truck."

They got out and went to the rear, where Johnny opened the back doors. Within, were the trussed up water inspectors, as well as the still unconscious Commissioner Gilz.

"You must have hit him pretty hard," Dan said.

"I only tapped," Steve protested. "He ought to be coming out of it any minute now."

"Well, we can't wait," said Dan.

Steve got some lengths of wire from the interior of the truck, and proceeded to tie the Commissioner securely. In the meantime, Johnny and Dan got their civilian clothes out of the truck, and changed over from the uniforms, which would no longer be of use to them.

Johnny laid the discarded uniforms down alongside the two water inspectors, who were watching everything with detached interest, not even making an effort to remove their gags, nor struggle at all.

Steve noted this strange attitude on their part, and asked Murdoch about it.

Dan grinned. "These boys are all right. We gave them each a hundred bucks out of our expense money, to sort of keep them happy. They say they'd like to do this seven days a week at that price."

"We could release them now," Steve said.

Dan Murdoch shook his head. "They want to be found tied up. They're afraid of what Gilz and those other police thugs would do to them if there was a suspicion they had allowed us to tie them up."

Steve finished gagging the unconscious Gilz with his own socks and garters, and then said to the water inspectors. "You boys can entertain him when he comes to!"

They waved to the two willing prisoners, and climbed down

off the truck. Johnny closed the back doors once more, and turned off the headlights. The truck was left in darkness.

"It'll be found pretty soon," he said. "They'll comb every street in town in the next couple of hours."

"Let's go, Mopes," said Stephen Klaw.

AS THEY walked west, he showed them the penciled telephone number on the cover of the Manning folder. "It's just possible that this is the number of the station house where they're holding Manning. Wait here and I'll go across to that candy store and look it up in the phone book."

He went into the store, and consulted the Directory. Under "Coast City—Police Department" he found a list of the Police Precincts. The number he was looking for was Winchester 4-3618. But it wasn't listed for any of the station houses. They were all under the single heading of police headquarters, and their calls cleared through the headquarters switchboard at Center I-1000.

Steve gave up in disgust, and went out again. "It's not in the book," he told Dan and Johnny. "We've got to try some other way of locating Manning."

"What about the other thing we're working on?" Johnny asked. "What about this Senator?"

Steve shrugged. "That's a blank wall, as far as we're concerned. There's no way we can find out why he wanted us to call off the investigation, outside of asking Jervis. So we might as well work on the Manning angle. Besides—" he grinned sheepishly—"I promised Martha I'd help her."

"Oh! So it's Martha and Steve now, is it? Ain't you the handsome Romeo! I thought that department was reserved for Dan!"

"Don't mind him, Steve," Dan Murdoch said soothingly. "He's just a jealous lug. Because no dame will even spare a second glance for that hulking hunk of horseflesh. Don't let him bother you at all. You just go ahead and marry the girl if you want to."

"Go to hell!" said Stephen Klaw, and started to walk away. "I'm going to find Fred Manning."

Johnny and Dan rushed after him, and each of them took an arm.

"Perish the thought!" Dan exclaimed. "We couldn't let Martha's little Stevie go off by himself and get hurt. We better stick close and see that nothing happens to you."

Steve grinned. "All right. When you two Mopes get through horsing around, maybe we can get some action."

They grew serious at once, and stopped their bantering.

Another block, and they came to a Diner.

"Let's go in here," said Steve. "We can get a cup of coffee while you phone."

There were a couple of cars parked in front of the diner, and the place was fairly well filled. As they stepped inside, they heard the radio blaring: *"The hue-and-cry is still in full swing for the gunmen who are still terrorizing the city. Their abduction of Commissioner Gilz, and a running fight with a squad car, climaxed an evening of ruthless depredations on the part of these thugs. It is now known that there are three of them, one posing as an attorney, and the other two as water inspectors. It is thought, however, that they must have discarded the water inspector masquerade by this time.*

"All avenues of exit from the city are watched. Escape is impossible. Orders have been issued to the police to shoot on sight. One of our most Public-spirited citizens—Yancey Jervis—has offered ten thousand dollars out of his own pocket, for the capture of these killers—dead or alive!"

The dining car was buzzing with conversation as Kerrigan, Murdoch and Klaw entered. Dan and Johnny sat down at the counter and ordered coffee, while Steve went over to the wall phone.

Steve dialed Tiffany 2-3647. He waited while the buzzer sound was repeated again and again. His eyes became bleak, and his lips tightened to a thin line. There was no answer.

At last he hung up, and made his way straight out of the Diner. Kerrigan and Murdoch followed in a minute, and met him outside. One look at his face told them there was trouble.

"What's up, Shrimp?" Dan demanded.

"Martha Manning doesn't answer her phone," Steve said.

"Let's go, then!" Kerrigan boomed.

CHAPTER 5
SUPER-SABOTAGE!

THEY GOT a cab, and five minutes later they were at Silver Street. They paid off the driver a block away from number 814, and walked the rest of the way. But they did not walk together. This was war, now. It was the kind of thing they knew all about, the kind of thing they did instinctively. They approached Martha Manning's building in the manner of an advancing army moving into hostile and possibly ambuscaded country.

Dan Murdoch faded down an alley to approach it from the rear. Stephen Klaw walked swiftly, carelessly, toward the front entrance. Across the street, in the shadows, Johnny Kerrigan covered him, with a gun in his hand.

Number 814 was a self-service elevator apartment house of the medium class.

There was a car parked in front of the door, with a man at the wheel and another one in the back. A third man was lounging against the doorway, smoking a cigarette.

Stephen Klaw seemed to pay no attention to them. With his hands dug deep in his coat pockets, he turned in to the entrance.

Immediately, the man with the cigarette moved over and barred his way, bringing a gun out. At the same time, both doors of the car came open, and the two men from within, leaped out. They rushed in to take Steve from the rear.

Klaw didn't turn around. He faced the man in front of him, who was thrusting a revolver into the pit of his stomach, with his finger tightening on the trigger. Klaw fired the right-hand automatic through the cloth, without taking it from his pocket. The slug took the man in chest, hurling him backward through the apartment house doorway. At the same time, a heavy gun began to blast from across the street. The two men who had come up behind Stephen Klaw threw up their hands, spun around, and crashed to the ground.

Johnny Kerrigan came running over, grim-faced, with his revolver smoking.

"Let's go, Johnny!" Steve shouted, and they ran inside.

From somewhere in the rear, another gun blasted twice. A moment later, Dan Murdoch appeared through the rear Service Entrance at the back of the foyer. His gun, too, was smoking.

"Nice trap," he said, looking at Steve. "Those guys figured you'd show up here when you called Martha Manning and she didn't answer. Only they didn't expect to have the tables turned on them. Better hurry. There won't be much time now. The cops will be on top of us in no time."

Steve nodded, and stepped into the elevator. Johnny Kerrigan and Dan Murdoch took their stand in the foyer, where they could cover the front door as well as the rear. They weren't taking any chances on Steve's escape being cut off when he came down.

Klaw slid the door of the cage shut, and sent it up to the third floor. Martha had told him she lived in apartment 3-A, and he went right to that door, with his right hand in his coat pocket.

The door was not locked. He kicked it open, and leaped inside, whirling as he came through the doorway. A black, shadowy figure loomed in the dark foyer, and a gun blasted almost in his face. The bullet sang its futile message of hate, nicking his ear. If he hadn't been coming in so fast, it would have caught him square in the face.

Steve fired from his pocket, and the dark figure toppled backward, into the corner behind the door. It remained there a moment, teetering, and then slid down to the floor.

STEVE DIDN'T stoop to inspect the body. He knew just

where he had hit that man. He had aimed for his heart, and he knew the fellow was dead.

He felt along the wall, found the electric light switch, and turned it on. Light flooded the foyer and the living room, and Steve sucked in his breath. Martha Manning had put up a fight, no doubt about it. A desk near the window was overturned, and the chair lay alongside it. The drapes had been pulled down from the window, and they lay in a little, pitiful heap on the floor. In the middle of the room there was a broken decanter, and the green rugs stained with a splotch of deep purple. Steve bent and smelled it. It wasn't blood. It was sherry from the decanter.

Of Martha Manning there was no trace. After he went through the bedroom and the bathroom, Steve breathed a sigh of relief. He had feared to find her body. He was glad to find that she had been taken away.

He knew that there wasn't any time to examine the room, but he threw a hasty glance around, and spotted a queer scrawl in vermilion, along the white baseboard next to the window. He stepped over there quickly. Strips of curtain lay here, discarded, and Klaw surmised that the hoodlums had used some of them to tie Martha Manning. She must have lain here while they tore the strips, and they had thought she was unconscious. But she hadn't been, for she had scrawled a message with her finger, wet from the Vermilion wine.

The message consisted only of a blurred telephone number, and if Steve hadn't seen that number before, he would never have recognized it.

It was Winchester 4-3618—the same number which was written on the cover of the Manning file!

He took one look at the number to check it and make sure it was the same. Then he sprang up and raced out of the apartment. Tenants were poking their heads out of other doors on the floor, but they quickly ducked in again when they saw him tearing out. He stepped in to the elevator cage and sent it scooting down to the main floor.

As he stepped out into the foyer he heard a heavy revolver explode, and then another and another. Kerrigan and Murdoch were at the front entrance, exchanging shots with uniformed men in the street. Just as Steve came into the foyer, he saw the rear Service Entrance open, and two men push in, with guns in their hands. They turned those guns upon the unsuspecting back of Kerrigan and Murdoch, but they never fired them, for Stephen Klaw's automatics both began to bark their dangerous dirge of death. The two attackers went down under his blasts, and Johnny and Dan turned around to see the finish.

Their own fight was over. They had wounded one of the uniformed men in the leg and the other in the arm, and there was no more fight left in them.

KERRIGAN, MURDOCH and Klaw raced out of the building to the police car out of which those two men had come. Johnny took the wheel once more, and sent the car speeding out of the block, just as another radio car siren came screaming from the other direction.

Steve told them swiftly what he had found upstairs.

"Jervis' crowd has Martha Manning at the same place where

they're holding her brother, Fred. We've got to locate it—Winchester 4-3615!"

"There's only one way to do it," Dan Murdoch said. "That's to ask the Telephone Company."

"We'd have to say we're G-men," Johnny objected, with his hands gripping the wheel, and his foot pressing down on the gas. "What about Senator Blank? What about his request—that we keep…"

"To hell with Senator Blank!" Steve snapped. "We've got to get to Martha and her brother!"

"Okay!" said Johnny. "I know just where the Telephone Company is. We passed it before."

No one thought to stop their police car as Johnny sent it speeding through the city streets. In less than five minutes he pulled up at the side entrance of the Telephone Company Building on Broadway. Johnny and Steve waited in the car while Dan Murdoch hurried inside. They were alert, watchful now. This was almost in the center of town, and there was plenty of excitement all about them. Police cars were scurrying past, and any one of them might stop to ask questions. Radios were blasting from every passing car, as people listened for more news of the three "desperados" who were terrorizing the town. Their own radio began to splutter, and then the headquarters announcer's voice came in staccato rhythm: *"Calling all cars! Go to East End. Shooting in Silver Street. Cooperate to bottle up district. Three desperados still at large. Remember orders—shoot at sight!"*

Just as the announcer finished and began to repeat the orders,

Dan Murdoch came out of the Telephone Building. He nodded, and crowded into the seat alongside Steve.

"I've got it!" he said. "Drive uptown, Johnny, and out on Route Two!"

As Kerrigan tooled the car up through traffic, passing red lights indiscriminately, Murdoch said crisply, "It's the airplane factory! The Manning Aircraft Corporation! The plant has been closed down by condemnation proceedings, and only a watchman appointed by the city has been on duty for the past week. They had the regular phone discontinued, and put in this private, unlisted wire!"

"Ah!" said Stephen Klaw. He took out his automatics and inserted fresh clips in them, while Dan Murdoch loaded his own two revolvers. Then Steve took Johnny's revolvers and inserted fresh cartridges for him.

"All set!" he said grimly.

CHAPTER 6
THE PRESSURE SYSTEM

THE MANNING AIRCRAFT CORPORA-TION was eight miles out of town, on Route Two. Johnny slowed up when they came over the last rise in the road, about a mile away. He switched off the headlights, and watched the white line in the center of the road as a guide. Johnny had done a lot of night driving without lights. He seemed to have a special, instinctive feel for the road.

Though there was not even a sliver of moon to increase visibility, he nosed that squad car down into the very shadow of the tall wire fence which encircled the Manning Aircraft grounds. The main factory building, and an auxiliary hangar for storing assembled planes prior to shipment, were down at the far end of the grounds. Between themselves and the building there was a wide landing field, equipped with beacons and landing lights, none of which were now in operation. A couple of lights shone in the windows of the auxiliary storage hangar.

Stephen Klaw pointed across the field toward the hangar.

"That's where we want to get, Johnny."

"Get the gate open," Johnny said, "and I'll take you there."

Steve nodded, and climbed out of the car. He walked over to the gate and inspected it. It was locked on the inside, securely fastened by a great bulldog padlock. Steve looked the padlock over for a moment. Then, extracting a certain instrument from his pocket, he deftly opened the lock. He grinned, and swung the gate wide open. Then he ran over and jumped on the running-board. Dan got on the opposite running board, and Johnny swung the car in through the gate. He kept the headlights off, and aimed straight for the auxiliary hangar.

Though he had been very careful not to warn those within the plant of their approach, Johnny made no effort at concealment when he reached the great rolling door of the hangar. Those doors were closed, but there was a small door at either side.

Dan and Steve jumped off the still moving car, and each of them made for one of those doors. Kerrigan brought the squad car to a stop and followed.

Dan Murdoch's door was locked, but one which Stephen

Klaw tried, gave under his hand. He pushed it open, while Dan and Johnny quietly joined him.

They stopped short in the shadows just inside, staring in amazement at that which was revealed within. At one side, the fuselages of six trim fighting planes were stacked in a row, occupying almost all of one wall. Opposite, there was the almost completed shape of a fully assembled Manning M-110. Near the door there was new machinery which had been delivered at the plant, but which there had apparently not been time to install before they were closed down by Jervis' order.

But it was not all this which claimed the attention of the three G-men. What held their eyes riveted in angry amazement was the scene in the center of the great floor. There lay the trussed-up form of a little girl, no more than ten years old. She was apparently drugged, for though she was breathing regularly, she did not attempt to move. Tied in a chair underneath a hoisting-hook, sat Martha Manning.

In another chair sat a thin, dark-haired young man who was unmistakably her brother. The resemblance was easy to notice in spite of the fact that Fred Manning had been pretty badly treated. There were cuts and lacerations about his face and upon the upper part of his body, which was stripped. He, too, was bound in the chair, and his head was sagging over weakly.

There were five men standing about them, apparently deeply absorbed in their work. Kerrigan and Murdoch and Klaw recognized all of them. Inspector Simpkin and Sergeant Wister were there, as well as two of the uniformed officials who had been present at the conference at Police Headquarters. The fifth man, none of them had seen tonight, but they had viewed pictures of him in Washington. He was Yancey Jervis!

SIMPKIN WAS standing behind Martha Manning's chair. He had the great hoisting hook in one hand. With his other he was forcing Martha's chin up.

"You talk now, Manning," he said to Martha's brother, "or you'll just sit here and watch your sister hoisted up in the air on this hook!"

The three G-men remained perfectly silent in the shadows, virtually invisible because of the bright light shining directly on the hideous scene.

Simpkin held the hook under Martha's throat, watching young Manning with the eyes of a hawk. Yancey Jervis was smoking a cigar, with furious intentness. He stepped over to Manning and grabbed him by the hair, yanking his head up.

"Look, damn you!" he growled. "Look at your sister! Look at that hook! Would you like to watch her hanging by it? It'll take her a while to die. You'll have to sit here all through it. Talk, you fool! Where did you hide that evidence?"

Manning appeared to be in possession of only half his senses. The torture to which they had subjected him during the last week must have weakened him terrifically.

"All right," he mumbled. "I'll—talk. I hid—"

"No, no, Fred!" Martha screamed. "Don't tell them. They'll kill us anyway. They'll never let us live. Because we know about little Nora French!"

Kerrigan, Murdoch and Klaw stiffened at the mention of the name of Nora French. So that little girl who was lying there

51

trussed up was Nora French. And the name of the senator who had begged them to cut short the investigation of Yancey Jervis was Abner French. No wonder that Senator French had almost begged on his bended knees!

Johnny Kerrigan growled deep in his throat, and took a quick, impulsive step forward. But Stephen Klaw seized his arm.

"Wait, Johnny," he whispered.

Martha Manning was still begging her brother not to talk, but Inspector Simpkin put a great hand over her mouth, stifling her. He kept the hoisting hook poised under her throat.

Yancey Jervis paid no attention to her. He was watching young Manning for the first sign of weakening. "You've got to understand, Manning, that this means a great deal to me. I won't stop at a thing like murder—"

"No, damn you. I know you won't!" Fred Manning screamed. "You've killed others already. And you stand to make a million dollars if you close down my factory. The Germans promised it to you if you stopped production of my planes for Britain! I have the proof of it! I have the letter from Doktor Schmitz. I have it hidden—"

"Exactly!" Jervis cut in smoothly. "And Doktor Schmitz is coming here tonight to be sure I've got the letter back. You understand, Manning, you must give it to me. It is important evidence. With that letter, I could be convicted as a saboteur, and Doktor Schmitz would be exposed as an agent of the German government. So you see, my friend, your sister's life won't stand in the way."

He turned and peered toward the door. "I believe Doktor Schmitz and his men have already arrived. Is that you—"

"No," Said Stephen Klaw, stepping forward into the light. "This isn't Doktor Schmitz!"

AT THE same time, Murdoch and Kerrigan fanned out on either side of him, and their guns began to speak in swift unison. Steve's two automatics cut down Yancey Jervis, while Kerrigan took care of Simpkin and his hoisting hook. Simpkin threw his hands up and fell backward, with two slugs through his throat, almost at the very spot where he had intended to insert the hoisting hook into Martha Manning's throat. Dan Murdoch, from the other side, sent a steady volley of slugs into the other men. Under that deadly hail of lead, fired from the guns of fighting men who had no mercy left in their hearts, the murderous and vicious crew of Yancey Jervis went down into utter extermination. The few straggling shots they managed to fire went wild, doing little damage—except for one bullet from the gun of Sergeant Wister. It was Kerrigan who got him, once in the shoulder, and once to the heart. He was spun around by that shoulder wound, and his gun went off by reflex action, though he was already dead on his feet. It was that bullet which smashed into the great drum of reserve gasoline at the far end of the hangar. There was a dull boom, and then great hungry tongues of flame shot upward, licking at the walls. In a moment, the rear of the great hangar was transformed into an inferno of roaring, fiery hell!

Swiftly, Stephen Klaw stooped and cut the bonds that held Martha Manning, while Kerrigan picked up the small, pitiful figure of little Nora French and carried her out to safety, two hundred feet from the hangar. Dan Murdoch slit at the bonds which held young Fred Manning, and had him free in a moment. Manning was now fully awake to the peril.

"The hangar!" he shouted. "I've got to get the chemical fire extinguisher. It can be stopped!"

He went careening crazily across the floor toward the small motor truck upon which was mounted the newly developed fire extinguisher capable of quelling all but the most advanced airplane fires. He mounted it and set the pump in motion, while Kerrigan and Murdoch ran to help him. Steve took Martha Manning by the hand and shouted above the throbbing roar of the fire, "Come on—I'll take you to the door!"

She started to follow him, but suddenly the terror and the strain which she had undergone took their toll. She wilted, and fell over in a dead faint.

Stephen Klaw cursed under his breath, picked her up in his arms. He started for the door and suddenly stopped short.

A small, compact group of men stood in that doorway, surveying the scene. These men all had the military bearing of men trained in the strictest and most ruthless army the civilized world has ever seen. In their lead stood a tall man with a monocle in his eyes, and a long-barreled Lüger pistol in his gloved hand. The others, behind him, all had guns ready for action.

At a word from their leader, they moved into the hangar with military precision. Their faces were cold, merciless.

The monocled man swung his gaze toward the spot where young Manning was driving the chemical fire truck toward the blaze, and already shooting the liquid chemical into the heat of the fire. He raised his gun to aim at Manning. That chemical extinguisher would certainly put the fire out, and these men didn't want it out. Killing young Manning would do the trick.

Steve cursed, and dug one hand into his pocket, grasped the automatic which lay there. There was still a slug or two in the magazine, but, burdened with the inert body of Martha Manning, he could not pull the automatic out. He fired through the cloth, and his shot took the monocled man in the side. The man went down and his followers, uttering a great cry of rage, turned their fire upon Klaw.

These men must have guessed their superiority in ammunition, for they advanced in open formation, firing leisurely. Steve fired the remaining cartridges in his gun, damning himself for not remembering that Jervis had been expecting Doktor Schmitz and his men. He could have been prepared for this. The price of unpreparedness might be death for all of them, including Martha Manning. He swung her down to the ground and pulled out his other automatic. He fired twice more before the hammer clicked emptily. There had been shooting from behind him, but that also stopped now. He knew that Kerrigan and Murdoch were also out of ammunition. Half a dozen of the attacking Germans were down, but the remaining four, with Doktor Schmitz, wounded but still directing them, would wipe out the Suicide Squad.

STEPHEN KLAW smiled. Well, they had been asking for this for a long time. Now that it was here, he could meet it with a smile. He folded his arms and waited.

Suddenly, there was a cry from the advancing Germans, and they swung their guns to the left. Startled, Steve turned in that direction. He let an involuntary cheer escape from his lips. Though the fire was still not entirely under control, the extinguisher had accomplished a good deal, by limiting the flame to the far end of the hangar. But Dan Murdoch had found another use for the extinguisher truck. He had pushed Fred Manning to one side, and was driving straight for the Germans. And the nozzles were spurting their chemicals in long, power-driven streams!

The Germans fired again and again, but they could hardly see their target, because the spray from the nozzle mouths formed a sort of smoke screen around Dan.

Stephen Klaw sprang forward, and suddenly found Johnny Kerrigan at his side.

"Wow!" yelled Johnny.

They stooped and picked up guns dropped by the wounded Germans, and sprang forward to the attack. There was little left to do but mop up what Dan Murdoch had begun. He kept the chemical truck in action only until he was sure his partners had the situation well in hand, then he turned it around and headed it back into the fire.

Kerrigan and Klaw took three prisoners, including the monocled Doktor Schmitz. The rest died under their guns.

Twenty-five minutes later, with the fire department on the scene, and the fire under control, Klaw turned the drugged, pitiful little figure of Senator French's daughter over to a nurse.

He let Martha Manning kiss him on the lips, then he turned

and looked sheepishly at Kerrigan and Murdoch. They winked at him solemnly, and turned and went out of the hangar. Steve's face grew red, and he squeezed Martha's hand and went out after them.

"Well, Stevie," Dan Murdoch said, "how do you like the taste of lipstick?"

"If you marry her," Johnny Kerrigan boomed, "you can settle down and make airplanes for the rest of your life. The girl must he worth a lot of dough. We'll come and see you once in a while—"

"If you two mopes would quit horsing around," Stephen Klaw growled, "we could get started back to Washington, and draw an assignment with some action!"

THE COFFIN BARRICADE

CHAPTER 1
ORDER FOUR COFFINS

DECEMBER THIRTIETH, Nineteen-forty. Two days before New Year's. It was a Monday. The schools were closed, but the banks and stores and theaters were open. Money was flowing freely, and all the liquor stores were crowded. The city was in a gay mood.

But there was no cheer in the little brownstone boarding house in the Seventies, just off West End Avenue. The black bit of ribbon on the door told its own grim story in the heart of a city given over to holiday festivities.

The funeral was over, but the long row of cars parked outside that modest building spoke much for the esteem in which the deceased must have been held; and meant that he had a great many good friends.

The license plates on those cars told another story, added another bit of information for the discerning passer-by. The car in front of the door was. *FBI 1*. Behind it was *DJ 2*, both District of Columbia. *FBI 1* belonged to the Chief of the Federal Bureau of Investigation. *DJ 2* was the official car of the Assistant Solicitor General of the United States, the assistant to the Head of the Department of Justice, of which the F.B.I. was an integral

60

THE COFFIN BARRICADE

part. There were other cars, belonging to state and national officials. A passing pedestrian might have wondered what brought all these important personages to the funeral of a person who had lived in such modest surroundings as the brainstorm that was Mother Kelly's Boarding House.

Inside, these important personages were gathered in the living room, talking in hushed tones. And on the first floor, in a small room which Mary Kelly used as an office, sat the owners of license plates *FBI 1* and *DJ 2*. Mother Kelly sat behind the old-fashioned, roll-top desk. She was dry-eyed, and her slim, frail body was erect. Her white hair was combed back tightly, and her dress was neat and fresh. But there was a faint streak of tear-stain upon each cheek.

On the wall directly behind her chair, there was a framed picture of a gray-haired man, strong-jawed, level-eyed. Underneath it, a small gold plaque which read:

INSPECTOR THOMAS KELLY
Federal Bureau of Investigation
United States Department of Justice
1889 – 1930
Presented by the Department of Justice in grateful
acknowledgement of the loyal services of a brave man who
gave up his life in the performance of his duty.
April 15, 1930

The Chief of the F.B.I. now held another framed picture in his hand. This was the picture of a younger man, but with the same strong jaw and level eyes.

"Mary," he said as he handed it to her, "you have been the wife and the mother of G-men. Ten years ago your husband died, and now it's your son. No woman has ever given more to her country. Whatever I say is meaningless in the face of your grief. Take this picture and this plaque and put them beside those others. May they help you bear your grief."

Mary Kelly took the picture and the plaque. For a moment, as she looked at the young man's portrait, her shoulders jerked. And then she carefully stood it on the desk. "Thank you."

The Assistant Solicitor General of the United States cleared his throat, He brushed irritably at his right eye, which seemed to be watering. "If there is anything you should ever need or want beside your pension, Mrs. Kelly, you have only to name it. We have a fund—"

She smiled wistfully. "There is nothing I need. This little boarding house gives me a living. All I ask of you is—" her frail hands clenched on the desk—"that you do everything possible to bring my son's murderers to justice!"

THE CHIEF of the F.B.I. threw a worried glance at his superior, the Assistant Solicitor General. "We must wait, Mary—"

"But why?" she cried earnestly, rising from her chair and standing over them. "You sent Tom after a criminal who called himself the 'Undertaker.' You sent him with another young, strong lad, named Jerry Nichols. But they never got the Undertaker. Instead, the Undertaker got *them*. He sent their bodies to us, in coffins, just as he has done so many times in the past, with others. In the morning, we found the coffin, with poor—Tom's body in it. And the Undertaker added his grim jest by—by preparing the body for—burial. Tom was—embalmed."

The Chief nodded. "I know, I know, Mary. I saw him. And I saw young Nichols, too. That makes eight. Eight men of the F.B.I. have gone after the Undertaker. All came back in coffins...." For the Undertaker had spies and agents everywhere. It was the strongest organization the F.B.I. had ever bucked. The Undertaker guaranteed protection to crooks, murderers, criminals of every description—and collected an assessment from them every month, like insurance. In return, he kept them out of jail. Every law-enforcement officer who arrested a criminal in the Undertaker's protection turned up in a coffin—embalmed and ready for burial. It was getting so that detectives were fearful of arresting a crook who carried one of those coffin-charms which identified him as being under the protection of the Undertaker!

Mother Kelly's eyes were flashing. "Then, why don't you do something? Why don't you throw every man of the F.B.I. into the job of getting the Undertaker?"

"We can't, Mary," the Chief said, miserably. "Ninety percent of our agents are working on sabotage and spy assignments. National Defense takes priority over everything else. We've got to keep our munitions plants from being blown up. And the Undertaker is aware of this. He's trading on it, counting on the fact that we can only send a few men after him."

"But—but—are you going to keep on pitting two or three men at a time against a powerful and ruthless organization? It—it's the same as—as suicide!"

"I know, I know. But—"

The Assistant Solicitor General raised a hand. "There's no other way, Mary. Congress wouldn't permit us to take men off National Defense assignments. And if we did, it would give foreign saboteurs an ideal chance to cripple the country. We've got to go on trying to get the Undertaker by assigning only a few men at a time—"

"You—you're going to—throw other men's lives away?"

"I'm going to try it just once more. I'm assigning three men—"

"Three more sacrifices!" Mother Kelly exclaimed. "What three men could succeed against the Undertaker?"

"The three men I have detailed to this job," the Director said with a faraway look in his eyes, "are eminently fitted for it. I should have given them the assignment in the first place—except that I needed them on other work. Now they're free, and I've asked them to come here. Lisbeth Nichols, the sister of poor young Jerry Nichols, saw the men in the hearse, who left her brother's body at their house Friday night. She can describe them, and identify them. She's in hiding now, lest the Undertaker find her and kill her before she can tell what she knows. I've talked with her on the telephone, and she wouldn't even tell *me* where she's hiding. But she said she would send a message to the three men I'm assigning, and make an appointment to meet them. With her help, those three may succeed where others have failed."

Mary Kelly gave him a queer look. "Would you care to tell me who those three men are?"

He nodded, smiling a little. "You've met them, Mary, and you know them. Their names are—Kerrigan, Murdoch and Klaw!"

"The Suicide Squad!" she exclaimed. "Johnny Kerrigan. Dan Murdoch. Stephen Klaw. They're willing to take the job?"

The Director said, "They're sore at me for not having assigned them to it in the first place. They're flying from Chicago tomorrow."

"I want to help them!" Mother Kelly said fiercely. "I want to help them avenge my son—and all the others. Tell them that. Tell them they can call on me for anything!"

NEITHER MOTHER Kelly nor the two men with whom she was talking was aware that their conversation was being overheard at that very moment. None of them was aware of the pseudo-mourner who had his ear glued to the door.

That man moved quickly away from the door as he heard Mother Kelly's two visitors rising to leave. He hurried down the stairs and went out through the long hallway, without entering the living room where the others were gathered. Furtively he made his way across to Broadway and stepped into a corner drugstore. He squeezed into a telephone booth and dialed a number.

"This is Number One-sixteen," he whispered into the phone. "Emergency report. Put me through, quick!"

Only a mile or so away—a couple of blocks west of Times Square—another man sat in an office on the first floor of a small, dignified looking building. On the stone front of that structure was chiselled the name: FLAMOND UNDERTAKING PARLORS.

THE COFFIN BARRICADE

From the outside, one would never have suspected the nature of the activities which went on within. The main funeral parlors were quiet and sedate, with a frock-coated manager who dealt courteously with any patrons who chanced to require their services. The business they did was substantial, and their prices were quite high. The Flamond Funeral Parlors enjoyed a very good reputation. But if any outsider had managed, by some accident, to pass through the strong steel door which shut off the cellar stairs, he would have been shocked beyond words. And he would have had a terrible story to tell—if he had ever succeeded in leaving the place alive.

For down here was a whole vast basement floor in which the real work was done. Here were secret embalming rooms which never saw the light of day. From here were taken the embalmed bodies of those law-officers who had been sentenced to death by the Undertaker. In one corner of the great basement there was a stack of caskets, collected secretly over a period of time, with all manufacturer's marks removed.

Weapons were stored here, and there was also a great vault with a time lock, where the daily proceeds of the Undertaker's widespread assessment system were kept.

Upstairs, on the first floor, was the office of Pierre Flamond, the directing genius of this efficient organization for the furtherance and protection of crime.

Flamond was a cadaverous-faced man, with white hair and great, bushy white eyebrows. His forehead was high and narrow, and his lips were thin. Dressed in his frock coat and his flowing bow tie, he presented to the world an appearance of deep-seated respectability.

THE MAN who sat opposite him in the office was Jonathan Jason, his attorney and fixer. Jason's position in the legal world was above suspicion, just as was that of his employer. No one knew that the many cases which Jason and his assistants handled in court were all referred to him by the Undertaker. His practice was generally thought to be wide and lucrative, and he had the reputation of always winning for his client. But today, Jason was palpably nervous.

"… but suppose the police should raid this place," he was saying. "The evidence they would find downstairs—"

"My dear Jason," Pierre Flamond interrupted, "you must do me the justice to believe that I have overlooked nothing. In the first place, this is the last spot in the world that the police would raid. And I will tell you why. Because the man they seek calls himself the Undertaker. They would hardly believe, therefore, that he is really in the undertaking business—"

"True, true," Jason said. "I'll admit that this is the cleverest masquerade ever conceived. But suppose one of your operatives were arrested and given the third degree? Under pressure, he might be forced to talk—"

"Never fear, my dear Jason. My operatives know that able lawyers will come at once to their assistance with writs of *habeas corpus*. And if the lawyers fail, there is always recourse to force. Already, half a dozen of my operatives have been taken out of jails by a mass attack."

Pierre Flamond leaned across the desk, his deep-set eyes

boring into the lawyer's. "Furthermore, Jason, everyone who works for me knows that if they talked—no matter how they were beaten or tortured—the immediate punishment would be death. I am satisfied, Jason, that no operative of mine will ever betray me." He stopped a moment, then said with slow deliberation: *"I am even sure of you, Jonathan Jason!"*

"Of course, of course," the lawyer said hastily. "You can depend on me, without question. But—but suppose the police should pick up some clue that would lead them here? You can't deny that such a thing might happen."

Flamond smiled crookedly. "In that case, Jason, the police would find nothing here."

"Ah!" said the lawyer. "You've got the basement mined!"

"Don't be too curious, Jason," Flamond said dangerously. "It is not quite healthy."

The lawyer grew pale. "I didn't mean anything. I—I only wanted to cooperate." He changed the subject quickly. "What about Lisbeth Nichols, the sister of that G-man who was embalmed together with young Tom Kelly? She saw your men on the hearse. Have you taken care of her?"

"Not yet," Flamond admitted. "She's smart. She's in hiding. I have two hundred operatives scouring the town for her. The trouble is, we don't know what she looks like. But we'll find her."

"If she should go to the F.B.I.—"

FLAMOND'S LIPS twisted. "I would like her to do that. The F.B.I. will place her in protective custody. And I will have one of my planes drop a demolition bomb on any building in which they keep her."

"That's a desperate resort—"

"But necessary. She saw the two men on the hearse. By the way—" Flamond looked queerly at the lawyer—"you know who one of those men was?"

For a moment, Jason was silent. A strange sort of tremor passed through his body. "Not—not my brother?"

The Undertaker smiled, and nodded. "Jock Cooligan, *alias* Noah Jason."

"Noah!" exclaimed the lawyer. "He promised me he'd lay low after his escape from the police. I told him I'd never be able to get him acquitted."

"Exactly. So he applied to me, and I engineered his rescue, as you know. Since then, he's been working for me."

"But—but why did you have to let him go out on that hearse?"

"Because Jerry Nichols had been after him. Nichols had a wanted poster, with your brother's picture. I deemed it only just that your brother should be the one to deliver his embalmed body!"

"Yes, yes. But—but if Lisbeth Nichols ever identifies him—"

"That is why we must find her quickly, Jason—"

He was interrupted by the ringing of the telephone. Flamond picked it up. "Yes?"

"It's Number One-sixteen, sir, with an emergency report," a voice said. "Shall I connect him?"

"Yes."

In a moment, One-sixteen was pouring his report into the telephone. Flamond's eyes began to glitter.

"Ah!" he said when the spy had finished. "Excellent work, One-sixteen. You shall receive a bonus this month."

He hung up, chuckling, and looked at Jason. "The Federal Bureau of Investigation is about to provide me with three more candidates for my coffins!"

Jason raised his eyebrows. "You mean they haven't learned their lesson yet?"

"It would seem so. They are sending three of their crack agents here from Chicago. Kerrigan, Murdoch and Klaw."

"The Suicide Squad!"

"Exactly!" purred Pierre Flamond. "The Suicide Squad. I am sure we can arrange it to their liking—their suicide!"

He flipped up a key on the enunciator box beside his desk, and said, "Instruct Number Nine to report for duty at once. Tell her that she will have fifty men to support her in this operation, and that I do not want her to fail. There are three G-men coming here tomorrow, and they will lead us to Lisbeth Nichols!"

He flipped down the key, and looked significantly at Jason.

"I think," he said softly, "that we shall need four coffins instead of three...."

CHAPTER 2
CORPSES FOR NEW YEAR'S EVE

A FEW horns were tooting, and the New Year's Eve crowds were thick on Broadway. Blue-coated policemen were stationed every hundred feet or so, and mounted officers on horseback worked hard to keep the throng on the sidewalks.

Somebody was waving a pillow case out of a hotel window, and everybody was happy and gay—everybody but Stephen Klaw.

Steve threaded his way morosely through the loud and effervescent gayety of Times Square, and turned east on one of the side streets. A big, husky drunk in evening clothes collided with him, and hung on for a moment, recovering his balance.

"Watch it, Shrimp," the big drunk whispered. "Don't you know you're being tailed."

Steve helped the big fellow to get his legs under him.

"I know it, Johnny," he said. "Two little greaseballs. Where the hell is Dan?"

"Covering the hotel. The girl hasn't shown up."

"Hell," said Steve. "If it wasn't for those two greaseballs, I'd think it was a bum steer."

The big drunk wabbled on his pins, and clung even harder to Steve for support. "Here they are, right up behind you. Want me to hold them so you can shake them?"

"Hell, no. Just bring up the rear."

Johnny Kerrigan hiccupped startingly, let go of Steve's coat, and staggered away, pushing through the crowd of pedestrians that flowed around them.

Steve continued on his way, heading for the Hotel Sovereign, fifty feet down the block. A henna-haired woman with a pasty face underneath a generous coating of rouge brushed by his shoulder and smiled at him.

"Happy New Year," she said.

"Same to you," Steve grunted, and kept going. The woman looked disappointed. The two greaseballs who were following

Steve passed by the woman, and she stooped swiftly and whispered into the ear of one of them. She jerked her head down the street, in the direction of big Johnny Kerrigan, who was bringing up the rear, still doing his drunk act.

The little dark-haired man turned swiftly and looked at Johnny, and his eyes glittered. He motioned to his companion and they both moved back toward Johnny Kerrigan. The henna-haired woman smiled cynically, turned and followed Stephen Klaw.

Steve appeared to be aware of what was happening behind him. He turned in at the entrance of the Hotel Sovereign without looking behind him. He heard a man scream, heard another utter a loud yelp of pain, and he smothered a grin.

The doorman slowed up the revolving doors for him, and smiled. "Happy New Year, sir."

"Same to you," Steve said. He passed through into the lobby.

Music was eddying up from the Scarlet Room in the basement, and more music was coming from the Regal Room at the rear. The lobby was thronged, and the taproom at the right of the lobby was doing a tremendous business.

Steve made his way through the jostling crowd of bare-shouldered women and freshly-barbared men, paying attention to none of them. He entered the taproom. The bar was solidly lined, and all the booths but one were filled. On the table of that unoccupied booth was a card which read, "Reserved."

Steve made for the empty booth.

A HOSTESS in a sheath-like black gown and a gilt tiara on her head stopped him.

"I'm sorry, sir, but this table is reserved—"

Steve looked at the gilt letters stitched on the left side of her bodice, which read, "Hotel Sovereign."

"I'm the party for whom the table is reserved," he told her.

She raised her eyebrows. "But it's being held for a Miss Nichols—"

"That's right. I'm to meet her here."

He took off his hat and coat, and slid into the seat.

"Then you're Mr. Klaw?" the hostess asked.

"That's right. Stephen Klaw. Suppose you bring me a brandy-and-soda while I'm waiting." He frowned. "Miss Nichols should be here by this time."

The hostess nodded. "She said she would be here at nine. It's a quarter after—"

"Is she a regular customer here?" Steve asked.

"No, sir. She sent a messenger at five o'clock, with a reservation. She asked for a table in the Regal Room, but this was all we had left."

"All right," said Steve. "She'll probably be along. Get me that drink, like a good girl."

"I'll tell your waitress, sir."

The hostess left, and Steve looked around the crowded taproom.

A couple of greasy-looking men at the bar had been watching him. They hastily turned away when they saw his glance sweep toward them. Steve gave no sign of noticing them.

A tall, slender man detached himself from the bar near the two greasy-looking customers and walked leisurely down along the booths toward the men's room at the rear. He came abreast of Stephen Klaw's table, jingling the change in the pocket of his tuxedo trousers. He brought his hand out with the change in it, and—apparently by accident—dropped two of the coins. They rolled under Steve's table, and the slender man uttered an angry exclamation. He bent down, searching for the money. As he did so, he said, "Hi, Shrimp. They've got the place covered from every angle. They're watching like hawks. I don't think the girl will dare to show up."

Steve picked up a menu and pretended to read it. It covered his face.

"I think these galoots are wise to you, Dan. They tried for Johnny, outside. I think he damaged a couple of them—from the sounds I heard. Look out for yourself."

"Don't worry about me," chuckled Dan Murdoch. "I'm just wondering if the girl will come."

"If she gets here," Steve said, "they'll try to knock her off."

Dan Murdoch crawled farther under the table, in search of a dime. "There must be a dozen of them around. We'd have a tough time getting her out."

"Well," said Steve, "hang around. Johnny should be right outside. The three of us ought to be able to take care of her."

Murdoch found his dime, got up, and dusted off his trousers. "The one break we get, is that these monkeys don't know what the Nichols girl looks like. But they'll know the minute she joins you at this booth. If we could only warn her—"

"Nuts," Steve broke in. "Better scram. Here comes my waitress."

DAN MURDOCH tossed the dime in the air, caught it, and strolled away, passing a beautiful blonde waitress who was carrying a tray with Steve's brandy-and-soda, and a dish of canapes. She was wearing the costume of an English tavern bar-girl, with a tight, high bodice, and a skirt that barely reached her knees. Her legs were shapely, and her body was firm, the skin of her face and throat full-textured and fresh. But as Steve glanced casually at her, he had the impression that she was working under a terrific strain. Her hand shook just a bit as she placed the brandy-and-soda on the table.

Steve looked up at her and smiled.

"Relax, sister," he said. "There's nothing to be nervous about. New Year's comes regularly every year. It'll all be over in the morning."

She threw a quick, scared look over her shoulder, then brought her eyes around to meet Steve's.

"You're right," she said huskily. "It'll be all over in the morning—if you don't get me out of here quick!"

Steve's hand was reaching for the brandy-and-soda. He stopped for a second, and then lifted the glass, covering up the beginning of an involuntary gesture of surprise.

"What do you mean, sister?"

"You're Stephen Klaw, aren't you?"

"Well?"

She forced a smile to her lips, to cover the deadly seriousness of her eyes. Then she said quickly, *"I'm Lisbeth Nichols!"*

Klaw's face was impassive. "You're a smart girl," he said. "How'd you get the costume?"

"I've been registered upstairs in the hotel," she told him hurriedly, "ever since nine o'clock this morning. I only went out long enough to send you the message to meet me here, and to send a Western Union messenger with a deposit and reservation for a table here for tonight. But *they* must have a spy here in the hotel. They found out about the reservation. When I came downstairs a few minutes ago I saw them—waiting like executioners to—to kill me. So I went around the back way, and bribed one of the waitresses to let me take her place tonight."

She bent over the menu which Steve was holding, as if she were pointing out to him the desirable dishes, or recommending something special. Her face was close to his, and Steve could hear her swift, excited breathing.

"Nice work," he said. "You've got grit, Lisbeth. Count on me for whatever you need."

"I'm afraid now," she breathed. "I—I don't know what to do next. I had to come in and warn you. But now—now I don't see anything to do but give up—"

"Don't give up yet," Stephen Klaw murmured. "You're not the kind to give up."

"But what can you, alone, do against these murderous thugs?"

"I'm not alone. But I can't do a thing if you quit on me. What room are you registered in?"

"Nine-o-nine. My sister is up there now, with a gun in her hand. The room is in her name—Mrs. Jane Meredith."

"All right," said Steve. "Go back to the kitchen. Act as naturally as you can. When you come back out here and find me gone, try to look surprised."

"Suppose—something happens to you up there?"

Steve laughed harshly. "There are a couple of friends of mine around here who will take over."

She looked into his eyes for a moment, and suddenly she smiled. "I know who those friends are. Kerrigan and Murdoch. The other two thirds of the Suicide Squad. All right, Mr. Stephen Klaw, I'm going to trust you. I'll fight them!"

THERE WAS new, fresh color in Lisbeth Nichols' cheeks as she picked up her tray and hurried back in the direction of the kitchen.

Klaw looked up and saw the henna-haired woman coming toward his booth. She stopped alongside the table and said, "Hello."

"Hello and good-by," Steve said sourly.

She laughed. "You're not very friendly." She put her handbag on the table and slid on to the bench opposite him. "Come on, don't be grumpy. Buy me a drink, won't you?"

Steve scowled. "Listen, I'm waiting for my wife. She's a very jealous woman. She always carries a gun and she's liable to shoot you if she finds you here. Why not scram?"

The woman laughed once more. She opened her bag, and put one hand in it. Steve saw something hard poke against the cloth, toward him.

"*I'm* the one that has the gun," the woman said softly. "And you're not waiting for your wife. You're waiting for Lisbeth Nichols. You probably realize that this is a trap for her. You perhaps intend to leave and try to warn her before she gets here. Well, you'll do nothing of the kind. I want you to sit very still—"

THE COFFIN BARRICADE

"Tut, tut," said Steve. He tipped his brandy glass, and flicked the contents at her dress.

Instinctively, she jerked away.

Stephen Klaw reached out in a lightning motion and grabbed the bag. His hand closed over it, pinioning her hand inside, together with the gun she was holding. He twisted a little, to turn the muzzle away from himself, then jerked the whole thing out of her grasp.

The woman's eyes blazed as she wiped the brandy-and-soda from her dress and coat. But she made no move to recover her bag.

Steve said, "Pardon me," and turned the bag upside down, dumping all its contents on the wet table. The gun was a small, twenty-two calibre pistol with a short, two-inch barrel. It was of Swiss manufacture, a make which Klaw had never seen before. But it looked businesslike enough for deadly work at close range.

"Nice little gun," he said, slipping it into his pocket. He spread out the rest of the stuff and raised his eyebrows at sight of a queer little charm made of black polished ebony and attached to a thin platinum chain. The charm was a miniature coffin, with the lid closed. Upon its face was engraved the number 9.

"Ah!" Steve said softly. "So you're Number Nine, eh?"

The woman tried to snatch the coffin-charm from him, but he slipped it into his pocket.

For a second, she seemed to be on the verge of springing at him. But she got control of herself and sat back in the chair, studying him.

"Mr. Klaw," she murmured, "you're a very foolhardy young man."

"Thank you," Steve said absently. He was fingering through the other things which had fallen from the bag. There was a card case containing engraved calling cards. The name on the cards was: *Wilma Manfred.*

"Wilma Manfred, eh?" he said. "And you work for the Undertaker."

She started visibly. "You—know about that?"

He laughed. "Everybody who carries these coffin-charms works for the Undertaker. You're Number Nine, so you must be pretty important. Right up near the top."

"Well?" she breathed, "what are you going to do about it?"

"I'm arresting you," he told her.

Before she realized what was happening, he had brought a pair of handcuffs up from under the table and slipped a bracelet around her right wrist. He snapped the other on his own left wrist.

SHE STARED at the handcuff in stunned silence. Then she raised her eyes to his. "Don't be a fool, Stephen Klaw. This place is full of the Undertaker's men. You'll never leave here alive—much less take me out with you."

He shrugged. "All right then, we'll see how you like being handcuffed to a corpse. Let's go!"

He started to get up, but she said hastily, "Wait. Wait just a moment."

"Well?"

"You must know that the Undertaker hates to have his operatives taken into custody. We operatives of the Undertaker never work alone. We have enough men here to blast you to death."

"I know," Steve said bitterly. "Last week, a young G-man by the name of Bill Nichols arrested Number Thirty-nine. He was shot down in the street five minutes after he made the arrest, and Number Thirty-nine was rescued. Bill Nichols died in the hospital—but not before he had managed to whisper a few words to his sister, Lisbeth."

The woman nodded. "And Lisbeth Nichols sent for you. But believe me, Stephen Klaw, she'll never tell you what she knows. The minute she appears here she'll be killed. And the minute you try to take me out of here, you'll be killed. Look!" She nodded in the direction of the bar. "Do you see what I mean?"

She must have given a signal of some sort, because half a dozen men were closing in on the booth. Some of them had come from the bar, others from the adjoining booths. And a few more were trickling in from the street entrance and the hotel lobby. The place was filling up with grim-faced operatives of the Undertaker, all in evening clothes. They were moving in silently, and each man had a hand in his pocket.

Hardly anyone in the taproom was aware of what was happening. The New Year's revelers were busy with their own fun, and if they noticed that surging body of well-dressed thugs, they thought it was some holiday prank.

Klaw's eyes were grey and cold. He rose to his feet, yanking the woman up by the handcuff. He slid both his hands into his pockets, dragging her wrist over toward him as he did so. He smiled.

"Well, boys," he said mildly, "what's holding up the show?"

They were close to the booth now, forming a sort of semi-circle in front of it. A couple of them brought guns out of their pockets.

A lantern-jawed man in the front rank of the thugs, looked at the bracelets linking Klaw's wrist to the woman's.

"The key!" he said softly, stepping closer, and thrusting a revolver at Klaw's stomach. "Give me the key."

Steve didn't appear to move. But his right hand came out of his pocket gripping one of his gunmetal automatics. It rose two feet in the air in a whip-lash motion and the sight struck the lantern jaw a sharp blow.

The man's mouth snapped shut under the impact of that *smack*. His head popped back and he collapsed. The others muttered oaths and surged forward.

"Kill him!" Wilma Manfred ordered fiercely.

But just then there was a strange interruption. Someone began to laugh.

CHAPTER 3
THE UNDERTAKER'S LEGIONS

I T WAS a strange, booming sort of laughter, like the deep-throated, Jovian hilarity of the gods. It rose above the strains of the music which seeped in from the orchestras in the Scarlet Room and the Regal Room, and it filled the taproom of the Hotel Sovereign. Those thugs were more startled by it than they would have been by a gunshot. Involuntarily, they turned to look. Johnny Kerrigan leaped up on the front end of the bar and started to kick away the glasses and bottles.

Kerrigan's laughter ceased abruptly. He stood there now, with a heavy revolver in each hand. He was no longer weaving on his feet.

"Happy New Year to you all!" he boomed. "Which of you rats wants to go out with the old year?"

Down at the rear of the taproom there was another sudden commotion, and the tall, lithe figure of Dan Murdoch leaped up on to, the bar. He, too, had a revolver in each hand. He was smiling, but there was a dangerous glitter in his dark eyes.

"Hi, Shrimp," he said.

"Hi, Mopes," said Stephen Klaw, from the booth.

Suddenly, one of the thugs shouted, *"It's the Suicide Squad! My God, the whole damned Suicide Squad is here!"*

"That's right," Murdoch said softly. "The Suicide Squad. Who wants to start the fireworks?"

"Shoot, you fools!" the woman shouted. "Shoot! They're only three against all of you. Shoot…"

Her voice died to a broken gasp as she saw the thugs fading away from the semicircle in front of the booth. As if by magic, a wide space opened in front of Steve's table.

There were few members of the Underworld who had not heard of Kerrigan and Murdoch and Klaw—the three Black Sheep of the F.B.I. who were never sent on a regular routine assignment, but who always rated the calls where death was almost a certainty. Not so long ago there had been five of them.

Then there had been four. Now there were only three. Tomorrow there might be two, one—or none.

Klaw bowed to the woman who was handcuffed to him. "Will you do me the honor to come along quietly, Wilma? Or shall I pick you up and carry you?"

The color had gone from her face, leaving it ghost-white under the rouge.

"I'll come," she said, very low. "These fools are afraid of you three. The Undertaker will deal with *them*. But there are others, outside, who won't be afraid. You'll never live to see 1941—none of you!"

Steve shrugged. He stepped around the table, and out of the booth. She went at his side, still watching a little hopefully for a move from the motionless thugs.

The other patrons in the taproom were looking on, wide-eyed and incredulous. They saw one slim and wiry man, who looked hardly more than a kid, leading a woman prisoner out through a crowd of gunmen, while his two companions held the wolves at bay.

KLAW GOT to the street door, and stopped there. Dan Murdoch ran down the length of the bar to where Johnny Kerrigan was standing, then turned and faced the mob once more.

"Okay, Johnny," he said.

Kerrigan then leaped off the bar, and went over to the door. He turned and faced into the room, with the two revolvers at his sides.

"Right, Dan," he called.

While Kerrigan covered him, Murdoch jumped down to

the floor, and walked to the door. Little was said among those three as they executed the maneuver. They had worked so long together that they could almost read each other's minds, and they functioned like a piece of smooth-running, well-oiled precision machinery.

Murdoch went through the revolving doors, out into the street. Then Klaw pulled Wilma Manfred through. Johnny Kerrigan waited, covering the thugs. Steve, on the outside now, stopped the movement of the revolving doors, and shouted, "Okay, Johnny!"

Kerrigan nodded, and backed out. Steve started the door moving again, and Kerrigan reached the street. Murdoch had already flagged a cab, and Klaw started to lead Wilma across the sidewalk. A small group of men was clustered fifty feet away, and one of them exclaimed, *"It's Number Nine! They've arrested Number Nine!"*

Guns began to bark as Klaw pushed the woman into the taxi-cab. Kerrigan and Murdoch swung to face the new attack, and their guns spoke in a blazing quartet of deep-toned thunder. Those four guns of theirs played a deadly symphony of doom for the thugs who were blasting at them. Erect and disdainful of the bullets that sang about their heads, they sent a withering barrage into the close-huddled group of gunmen.

From the Hotel Sovereign, several of the thugs came barging out to join the fray. Kerrigan and Murdoch were facing down the street, and to those jackals from the taproom it seemed to be a good opportunity to take the two G-men in the flank. But they had reckoned without Stephen Klaw.

In the taxicab, Klaw thrust the woman into the seat, holding her there by the one manacled hand. With the other, he fired his automatic nine times at the surging mass of men who were fighting to come through the revolving doors. Glass shattered and men screamed as Klaw's lead mowed them down and drove them back upon those behind. The throngs of pleasure-seeking pedestrians scattered, leaving the field of battle to the fighters.

But it was over almost as soon as it began. More than half of the Undertaker's gunmen lay dead in the street. The rest lost their desire for the fight. They turned and ran.

Kerrigan and Murdoch lowered their empty, smoking guns, turned and looked at each other.

"Nice work, Mr. Kerrigan," said Dan.

"Thank you, Mr. Murdoch," Johnny said, "and the same to you."

Stephen Klaw grunted impatiently. "Will you two Mopes stop patting yourselves on the back? We're losing money while this cab waits. Can't you see the flag is down?"

They both turned solemnly and bowed to Steve.

"Sorry, Mr. Klaw," they said in chorus, and climbed into the cab.

The driver looked a little sick.

"Now 1-listen, gents," he quavered. "My draft number ain't been called yet. I d-don't wanna get knocked off before I even join the army—"

"It's all over, Oscar," Steve told him, as he saw the name Oscar Hammer on the card in its metal frame. "Nobody will shoot at us for a while now. Get going up Eighth Avenue, fast."

"Sh-shouldn't we w-wait for the cops?"

"*We* are the cops!" Dan Murdoch told him, poking his badge out under his nose. "See?"

"Oh! I s-see," Oscar stuttered, and his big foot tramped on the gas.

HE WAS so nervous that the cab jerked and bucked for ten feet before he got it going. But then he really gave her the gun, and dodged and twisted through the traffic like one possessed.

Kerrigan and Murdoch reloaded their revolvers while Stephen Klaw unlocked the handcuff from his wrist. Wilma Manfred was dazed. She kept looking from one to the other of them, as if unable to believe that they were all still alive. Time and again she had witnessed the ruthless manner in which the deadly and efficient gunmen of the Undertaker had disposed of opposition. She could not yet understand why the superior numbers of the gunmen had been routed by these three men.

She offered no resistance when Klaw transferred the bracelet from his own wrist to her left wrist. Now both her hands were cuffed.

Steve handed the key to Kerrigan.

"Take her up to Mother Kelly's, Johnny. Hold her there incommunicado. Maybe she'll decide to talk."

Wilma Manfred looked at him dully. "You're not taking me to the police station? You're not booking me?"

Steve laughed harshly. "You want to be booked, eh? So one of the Undertaker's lawyers can bail you out, or get a writ of *habeas corpus!* Well, lady, the answer is no. We're going to keep you out of circulation till we clean up Mr. Undertaker. You're too dangerous."

She had a beaten look in her eyes. "I—can't believe it. This can't be happening. No operative of the Undertaker has ever failed to get free. The Undertaker guarantees it."

"This is one time," Dan Murdoch chuckled, "when the Undertaker's guarantee is only worth thirty cents on the dollar." He looked at Steve. "Have you got the play, Shrimp?"

Klaw nodded. "I contacted Lisbeth Nichols. I know where to find her."

"Ah!" said Johnny Kerrigan. "I get it!"

Wilma Manfred looked incredulous. "That's impossible. I had my eye on you every minute of the time. Lisbeth Nichols didn't show up. And you talked to no one except Murdoch, here and the hostess and the waitress—" She stopped abruptly, and a light flickered across her eyes. "I see! One of those girls was Lisbeth Nichols!"

Steve nodded approvingly. "Smart girl. Now, if you could only get to the Undertaker and tell him—"

Murdoch leaned forward through the connecting window and gave Oscar directions for reaching Mother Kelly's. Then he turned around in the folding seat, next to Johnny Kerrigan, and faced Steve.

"One of us will have to stay with Wilma at Mother Kelly's," he said.

Steve nodded. "That's right. And it can't be me."

"Hell," said Johnny, "you always get the breaks."

"Wait a minute," said Dan. "We could lock her in Mother

Kelly's attic room, the one with the shutters. And we could leave Oscar on guard outside the door. Mother Kelly would stay with him—"

"Wait," said Murdoch. "I'll talk to him."

THE CAB was just pulling up in front of the three-story brownstone boarding house, where the bit of crepe still hung alongside the door.

Murdoch was busy explaining to the driver, "It's like this, Oscar. I'm Murdoch, and these are my partners, Kerrigan and Klaw—"

"Yeah," said Oscar. "I know all about you guys. They call you the Suicide Squad. I never could figure out how you got that label. But just now, I seen why. Boy, the British ought to have you three guys. They'd lick Hitler over night—"

"Thanks," said Murdoch. "But they won't let us go. Now listen, there's something you could do to help us—"

"Name it, Mr. Murdoch. I ain't much for talking, but my dough is on you three guys."

"Fine. Now we've got this dame here, and she's a sort of white elephant on our hands. We can't take her to a station house or to the Federal Court and book her, because the Undertaker would get his lawyers in there to free her, or else he'd send a small army of gunmen to blast her out of jail. He's done that already, a half dozen times."

"Yeah, I know. I read in the papers how he bombed a court house in Indiana—"

"So we want to keep this lady under cover. We can do it here, in Mother Kelly's. But one of us would have to stay with her—unless you were willing to do it—"

"Say no more, Mr. Murdoch!" Oscar exclaimed dramatically. "Just give me a gun."

"Mother Kelly will give you one," Johnny Kerrigan said. "She has a small arsenal in there."

"Let's go," said Steve Klaw.

CHAPTER 4
THE SUCKER TEST

FIFTEEN MINUTES later, the taxicab was speeding south on Eighth Avenue again. Only this time, Johnny Kerrigan was at the wheel, wearing Oscar Hammer's cap and hack badge. Dan Murdoch and Stephen Klaw were his passengers.

Back at Mother Kelly's, Oscar Hammer was in seventh heaven, sitting with a gun in his lap outside the door of the attic room in which they had locked Wilma Manfred. They had taken the extra precaution of handcuffing one of her wrists to the bedframe, so there was little chance of her escaping by her own devices. The only danger was that they had been followed to Mother Kelly's by some of the Undertaker's men. But this was so remote a possibility that Mother Kelly had been willing to chance it. She herself was sitting in the parlor downstairs, by the window, with a shotgun beside her.

"And good luck to you boys," she had said at parting. "Strike a blow for—young Tommy!"

There were tears in her eyes as she watched them drive away.

"We'll strike a blow for Tommy, all right!" Dan Murdoch said grimly. "If we can only get to the Undertaker!"

Johnny Kerrigan parked the cab on Ninth Avenue, and they walked the block across to the Hotel Sovereign. The crowds were becoming thicker and wilder as midnight approached. It was going to be a big New Year's all right, from every angle. And the Undertaker would get in his licks tonight, too. During the past year he had built up an organization that was virtually invulnerable to all law-enforcing efforts. Criminals everywhere, plying their trades tonight among the gay, hilarious throngs, would rob and murder with impunity, knowing that the tithe of their takings which they paid to the Undertaker would guarantee them safety.

The assessments these crooks paid to the patron devil were heavy, but they were worth it to them. And the Undertaker's reapings from tonight's sweep of crime would be gigantic.

Somewhere in the city that unknown ghoul sat chuckling, safe behind the impregnable wall of the criminal army of thugs he had built up. And to him, the three men who sought him must have seemed a very small worry indeed....

THE CROWDS thickened as Kerrigan and Murdoch and Klaw approached the hotel. They saw that the police had roped off a large area in front of the building. The bodies of the Undertaker's gunmen had not yet been removed. The Medical Examiner's staff and the Homicide men were measuring and marking off the spots where the bodies lay. No one was permitted to enter or leave the Sovereign.

"Well," said Kerrigan, "how do we get up to Room Nine-o-nine?"

"There's Inspector Hansen, of Homicide," Murdoch said. "We could take him aside and tell him about it."

"Nix," Steve vetoed. "There must be plenty of the Undertaker's spies hanging around there. Let's keep as far away as possible. We don't want them on our tail now. The idea is to talk to Lisbeth Nichols without giving the Undertaker's men a chance to get at her."

"Were you looking for me?" a clear young voice asked, behind them.

"Well, I'll be damned!" said Stephen Klaw, turning around. "Boys," he said, "meet Lisbeth Nichols!"

She smiled at Kerrigan and Murdoch. "I ran out through the kitchen exit when I saw you three shooting it out with that crowd in the street. I knew the police would sew up the hotel in a few minutes, and I'd be caught inside. I thought you'd be coming back to find me, so I hung around out here."

She was still wearing her short-skirted waitress's uniform, with a fur coat thrown over it.

"Let's get out of here, quick!" Stephen Klaw said.

He took her by the arm and led her back toward Eighth Avenue. Dan Murdoch went ahead, and Johnny Kerrigan trailed, just in case any of the Undertaker's gunmen should recognize Steve and start anything.

Horns were blowing all around them and close-packed people were shouting good-naturedly to each other. It still lacked an hour of midnight, and the revelers were getting themselves in the right mood for the end of the old year.

There was a little Coffee Pot down near the corner of Eighth Avenue, and Steve took Lisbeth Nichols in there, and ushered her to a booth. Johnny Kerrigan and Dan Murdoch followed them in, and joined them. Steve pulled down the Venetian blind over the window so that they could not be seen from the street. Dan Murdoch, who sat facing the door, took a gun out of his holster and kept it in his lap. His eyes never left the door.

"Four coffees," Kerrigan told the waiter.

Lisbeth Nichols looked from one to the other of them. "I—I never expected to see all three of you alive again. I thought—if just one of you survived that gunfight outside the Sovereign, it would be miraculous."

"We have a lease on life," Murdoch told her with a crooked smile, "until we get the Undertaker."

Lisbeth's sensitive face immediately clouded. "My brother, Jerry, needs to be avenged. And so does Tom Kelly—and all the others."

"What can you tell us that will help?" Stephen Klaw asked.

"Only this. I saw both men on that hearse Friday night—or, rather, three o'clock Saturday morning. I hadn't been able to sleep, and I heard a noise outside. I went to look out the window. Those men had already left the coffin at the door, and they were climbing up into the hearse to drive away. I saw their faces clearly, but I didn't see the coffin. After they drove away, I looked down to the stoop and saw the black box. But the hearse was gone."

"I see," said Steve. "And you could identify these men if you met them again?"

"Yes!"

Klaw looked glum. "All we have to do is find them, huh?"

"No, no!" she said eagerly. "I recognized one of them. It's a criminal named Cooligan. Jock Cooligan. My brother, Jerry, used to bring "wanted" posters home, and he used to let me look through them. I remember distinctly, seeing the face of this Jock Cooligan on one of them. He was wanted for murder. It was easy to recognize him, because he had a crooked nose, and a scar running from his lip down to the cleft of his chin. I'm sure it was Cooligan!"

KERRIGAN NODDED. His memory for faces was prodigious. "Jock Cooligan, *alias* Noah Jason. His brother is the well-known criminal lawyer, Jonathan Jason. Noah was the black sheep of the family. Jonathan was going to defend his brother on the murder charge, but Noah escaped when the car in which he was being taken to court was sideswiped by a hearse. Happened a year ago last May, and no one has ever seen Jock Cooligan, *alias* Noah Jason, since then."

"You think Jonathan Jason would know where his brother is hiding out?" Murdoch asked.

"I doubt it," said Johnny. "Jonathan's reputation is pretty good. He even stated publicly that if he knew where Noah was, he'd turn him over to the police."

"H'm," said Stephen Klaw. "You can never tell by what a guy says. Let's give this Jason guy a whirl."

"The sucker test?" Murdoch asked.

Steve nodded.

Lisbeth Nichols looked puzzled. "The sucker test? What's that?"

"Wait and see," Klaw said cryptically.

Murdoch got up and went to the phone booth. He looked up a number in the book, scribbled it on a bit of paper, and brought it back. "That's his address," he said. "Hudson River Terrace, West Fifty-first Street. And his phone number."

Kerrigan got up, took the paper and tore off the telephone number. He put the phone number on the table.

"Okay, Shrimp. Give us fifteen minutes. It'll take that long for us to get over there in these crowds.

Klaw nodded. Kerrigan and Murdoch went out.

"But I don't understand," Lisbeth Nichols protested.

Klaw grinned. "It's a little system we work when we need to check on a guy. Come on, have another cup of coffee while we wait."

At the end of fifteen minutes, Klaw got up and went over to the telephone. He dialed the number which Murdoch had scribbled down. Lisbeth Nichols came close to him, so she could hear what was said.

"Mr. Jason?" Steve asked. "Mr. Jonathan Jason?"

"This is Mr. Jason," an irritable voice replied. "What is it?"

"I should like to see you at once, sir. May I come over?"

"Well—er—I was just going out to a New Year's party. Who are you? What do you want?"

"I am Stephen Klaw, Special Agent of the Federal Bureau of Investigation."

There was the sound of a suppressed gasp at the other end. "Klaw!" A moment of silence followed, then Jason hurried on, in a more normal voice. "I've heard of the name. What did you want to see me about?"

"I have reason to believe that your brother, Noah, is involved with the Undertaker."

"Impossible! I don't believe it!"

"I have information that tends to prove it."

"Just what is this information?"

"I would prefer to tell you in person."

"Have you told anyone else about this, Mr. Klaw?"

"Not yet. I thought I'd wait and talk to you before reporting to Washington."

"In that case—" Jason's voice was almost eager—"can you come over in about fifteen minutes?"

"Thank you. I'll be there."

Klaw hung up and grinned at Lisbeth. "I think we've hooked him. Let's go!"

"But what's the sucker test?" she demanded as he hurried her out of the coffee pot, into the crowds swirling along Eighth Avenue. "How does it work? All I can see is that you've exposed yourself to terrible danger—if Jonathan Jason is really working with the Undertaker."

"That's the idea." Steve explained. "If Jonathan knows where Noah is, and if he's protecting his brother and working with the Undertaker, then we're giving him a chance to make a sucker of himself—by nibbling at our bait!"

IT TOOK them the full fifteen minutes to get over to the

Hudson River Terrace, on West Fifty-first Street. Lisbeth looked around in search of Kerrigan and Murdoch, but she didn't see them. Steve had hold of her arm with one hand, but he kept the other hand in his pocket as he steered her straight into the swank entrance.

The doorman was not in evidence.

Steve was alert, watchful. He led the way across the spacious foyer to the door of the elevator, which was closed. The indicator showed the cage to be at the ninth floor. Steve turned and stood with his back to the wall, both hands in his pockets now.

"Press the elevator button four times quickly," he told Lisbeth Nichols, "and then three times, slowly."

Puzzled, she obeyed.

Immediately, the indicator began moving down. In a moment the cage reached the ground floor and the door slid open. Johnny Kerrigan grinned at them from the controls. In the corner cowered the uniformed doorman, and the elevator operator, goggling at the heavy service revolver with which Johnny was keeping them covered.

Steve pushed Lisbeth into the cage and Johnny closed the door and sent it up again.

"I see it worked," Steve said.

Johnny nodded. "Right on schedule. Dan and I herded these two bozos up with us, and we made 'em use a pass-key to open Jason's apartment door. Dan kept these guys quiet while I moseyed in. Jason was just hanging up on you, and he didn't wait a second. He dialed another number. I jumped him and clicked the phone down, so the party at the other end must have thought it was a mistake."

"Did you get the number he dialled?" Klaw asked.

"Sure did," said Johnny.

He opened the door at the ninth floor, and shoved the doorman and elevator operator ahead of them to Jason's apartment.

Dan Murdoch was sitting on the lawyer's stomach when they came in. Jason was wearing a beautiful black eye and a split lip.

"Can you imagine it?" Dan said indignantly. "He tried to make a break. He grabbed for a gun in his desk, and I had to smack Mr. Jason a couple of times."

"Hello, Mr. Jason," Stephen Klaw said. "Haven't we an appointment?"

"This is an outrage!" Jason gasped, wriggling under the weight of Murdoch's lanky form. "You have no right to do this to me!"

"Of course not," Kerrigan said soothingly. "We ought to be ashamed of ourselves!"

He gave Steve a slip of paper on which there was a memorandum. "I checked with the phone company on the number he called. This is what they gave me."

Klaw raised his eyebrows when he read, *"Flamond Funeral Parlors."*

"This is rich," he said. "The Undertaker has really been an undertaker all the time!"

"You're mad!" Jonathan Jason cried, from his position on the floor. "You're mad to think that Flamond is the Undertaker. He's a respectable business man—"

"Then why did you phone him as soon as you hung up on Klaw?" Kerrigan demanded.

"I—I merely wanted to talk to him. He—he's a friend of mine."

"Sure," said Johnny. "You just wanted to wish him a Happy New Year!"

Stephen Klaw grunted. "Wrap him," he said. "And the other two guys, also. We'll leave them here while we go New Year's calling!"

CHAPTER 5
CUSTOMERS FOR COFFINS

THE VENETIAN blinds were drawn all the way down over the main floor windows of the Flamond Funeral Parlors as Stephen Klaw approached the place, walking on the opposite side of the street. But he saw that there was a light in a window on the upper floor.

Klaw walked to the next corner, crossed the street and came back. When he was about halfway up the block, a slowly moving taxicab passed him. Kerrigan was behind the wheel, and Murdoch in the back. They had once more picked up Oscar Hammer's cab. Steve nodded to them, and Johnny drove a few feet past the Funeral Parlor, and pulled in to the curb.

Steve went up to the door. There was a button alongside it, and a sign which said, *"Ring bell for all-night service."*

Stephen Klaw rang the bell.

It was deadly quiet on the street while he waited there. Only a few blocks away, the tempo of the New Year's revels was rising to a new high crescendo as midnight came close. But here, off the beaten path of amusement, there was no one.

Footsteps sounded inside and a dim light shone through. Someone was fumbling with the lock. It clicked, and the door came open. A man stood there, but he was partly hidden by the door. And Klaw knew that the man was not alone, for there was a shuffling behind him, as of other men moving into position.

The fellow who had opened the door was squat, with a low forehead and close-cropped hair.

"What is it?" he asked.

"I'd like to see Mr. Flamond." Steve had both hands in his pockets now, and he stood close to the opening.

"Mr. Flamond? Who wants to see him?"

"Tell him it's Stephen Klaw, Special Agent of the Federal Bureau of Investigation."

The fellow's eyes narrowed. "What did you want to see him about?"

"Well," Steve drawled, "I heard he had a coffin ready for me."

The fellow said, "Ar-gh!" and brought a gun out from behind the door.

Klaw didn't take his hands out of his pockets. He fired the right hand automatic through the cloth and hit the man in the stomach. His automatic's bark was muffled by the cloth, and the wounded man's scream was louder than the report.

Steve launched himself forward in a driving thrust and struck the door hard with his shoulder, smashing it backward, into the men who were hiding behind it. Then he was inside.

He swung around, and in the dim light he saw three men who sprang out from the shelter of the door, with guns in their hands. Steve had his automatics out now. He pulled the trigger of each, three times quickly in succession, and his slugs slammed into those gunmen at close range, with sledgehammer force. They were slapped back against the wall before they could fire a shot.

Now, Kerrigan and Murdoch came charging in, with their revolvers out. A door in the rear of the showroom was opening, and men began to spew forth. They were all armed, and viciously desperate. Their guns began to blast.

Kerrigan and Murdoch and Klaw moved toward that upsurging mob, shoulder to shoulder, firing in synchronized unison, sending a steady barrage of death into those gunmen. The leaders fell under the accurate, withering fire, and the others turned and raced back down the basement stairs.

"Johnny and I will take them, Shrimp," Murdoch shouted. "You get upstairs and look for the boss!"

He and Kerrigan raced down the stairs after the retreating thugs, their guns still thundering.

STEPHEN KLAW turned and sped toward the left side of the showroom where another staircase led to the second floor. He took those stairs two at a time, and reached the next floor just in time to see an office door opening. He glimpsed the gaunt-featured Pierre Flamond, and then the door was slammed shut.

Two shots smashed through the panel, waist high. But he had already dropped to one knee, and the bullets missed his head by a scant inch.

Steve placed one of his automatics at a slant, pointing at the lock, and emptied the gun, firing the six remaining shots into a circle about an inch in diameter. Then he sprang up, to one side, and kicked the door open.

He went into that office like a tornado and snapped a shot at Pierre Flamond, who was firing from behind his desk. Flamond's shots were hasty and wild. They spattered the wall behind Steve, and some of them sang into the hallway, through the wide-open doorway. Steve's shot smashed Flamond's right shoulder. He cried out, and dropped the gun. Then he rose slowly to his feet.

"Don't shoot!" he called out.

Steve lowered his gun and took a step forward.

Flamond uttered a hoarse cry of triumph, and raised his left hand and grasped hold of a switch in an open switch-box on the wall right in back of the desk. The switch was a foot above his head, and he gripped it hard, turning a ghastly smile of vicious hatred upon Steve.

"Remain right where you are!" Flamond barked. "If you value the lives of your two friends, do not move!"

Steve stood very still, the automatic lowered at his side.

"What's the play, Mr. Undertaker?" he demanded.

"You are clever enough to understand. If you should shoot me again, I will fall. But I will pull this switch down with me, and close the circuit, which will automatically set off an incendiary explosive in the basement. Your two friends will perish in a raging chemical fire, calculated to destroy everything down there. Do you see the point, Mr. Klaw?"

"I see the point," Klaw answered. "I also see a fuse-box!"

As he spoke he raised his automatic and fired four shots into the four fuses in the box over in the far corner. He saw Flamond frantically drag the switch down, and he prayed that he hadn't missed the fuse which controlled the explosive current.

All the lights in the office abruptly went out. Deep, impenetrable darkness moved in on the place. And at the same time he heard a sharp, crackling explosion from somewhere down below in the bowels of the building.

Steve uttered an exclamation of horror. He had been a split-second too late. That switch had closed the current for just long enough to set off the charge down there. Kerrigan and Murdoch were trapped.

Steve dragged out his fountain pen flashlight and snapped it on, cursing. He swung the beam toward the desk and fixed it on Flamond, who was stooping to pick up his gun, with his left hand. The Undertaker brought the weapon up. His face was twisted in a horrible death's head grin.

Klaw waited until the gun was level. Then, tight lipped, he fired once. His shot carried away the top of Pierre Flamond's head. The bloody mess was limned for a second in the beam of the flashlight, and then it disappeared behind the desk.

Steve whirled about, and raced out into the hall. He took the steps down recklessly, lancing his flashlight ray ahead of him. Down on the main floor, he could hear fire crackling below. Dense, pungent fumes were coming up through that open basement door. Men were screaming down there, and shots were blasting. Somewhere outside, a siren wailed.

STEVE RELOADED his guns and raced down those

cellar steps, reached the bottom, and stopped short. Flames were leaping high, almost in his face. At the far end of the basement, Kerrigan and Murdoch were barricaded behind the pile of coffins which the Undertaker had prepared for his victims. At the other end, was a group of perhaps fifteen of the gunmen, shielding themselves behind casks of embalming fluid, and piles of hearse blankets. They were keeping up a continuous fire into the barricade of coffins, and at the same time they were trying to edge around the dancing flames, toward the stairs. Kerrigan and Murdoch were making no attempt to escape. But they were covering that open space between the thugs and the stairs, so that none of the gunmen might escape.

Steve raced around the edge of the raging fire, and leaped behind the barricade to join Kerrigan and Murdoch.

"Hi, Mopes," he shouted. "I thought you were cremated by this time."

"We're too hot to burn!" Murdoch yelled. "We were keeping these bozos down here for fear they might get upstairs and cramp your act."

"The show's over," Klaw told them. "Pierre Flamond has no top to his head."

"In that case," Johnny Kerrigan boomed, emptying his revolver into the gunmen, "what's keeping us here?"

He stood up, the upper part of his body exposed above the barricade, to the fire of the gunmen. Disregarding the whining slugs, he shouted, "Listen, you muggs. Flamond is dead. Throw down your guns and surrender and we'll let you out of here. Otherwise, you stay down here, and get cremated!"

"To hell wit' you!" screamed one of the thugs. "You'll get burned alive too. You ain't got the nerve to keep us down here—"

"They have, they have!" shouted another of the gunmen. "It's the Suicide Squad! They don't give a damn. I'm quittin'!"

He jumped up, threw down his gun, and raised his hands in the air.

The firing ceased. With the fire raging less than ten feet from them, those gunmen rose, one by one, and threw away their weapons. In two minutes, they were all standing there with their hands up.

Kerrigan winked at Murdoch and Klaw. "It pays to have a reputation, I guess! Go ahead, Shrimp. Get upstairs, and cover them as they come up."

Klaw nodded, and raced back around the fire, to the stairs.

"One at a time!" he shouted. "Come on, and snap it up!"

The gunmen came, eager, glad to get out of the raging inferno, even at the cost of their liberty. Klaw herded them up, and Kerrigan and Murdoch waited till the last of them had left, then followed. They didn't get out any too soon. As it was, Johnny had to beat out a fire that caught at Murdoch's coat.

Up in the showroom, they herded the thugs out into the street, just as the first of the police cars raced up, siren shrieking. In a few moments the street was filled with police cars and fire apparatus. But the building which had housed the Flamond Funeral Parlors was doomed—along with the body of Pierre Flamond.

Inspector Hansen of Homicide arrived, and Klaw told him

the set-up, as swiftly as possible. He turned the prisoners over to Hansen, for there would be as many local charges against them.

"After you get through throwing the book at these boys," Murdoch said, "we want them. We have a whole encyclopedia to throw at them!"

Steve Klaw looked at Kerrigan and Murdoch, and then he looked at his watch. "It's twenty-five minutes of twelve, Mopes," he said. "We have a prisoner at Mother Kelly's to turn in. Besides, Lisbeth Nichols and Mother Kelly might feel a little more like welcoming the New Year if they knew we'd settled a score for Tom Kelly and young Nichols."

"Good idea," said Dan. "Let's go."

"Wait a minute," Johnny Kerrigan protested. "Shouldn't we call up the Chief and report?"

"Aw hell," said Dan Murdoch. "We'll call the Chief next year!"

THE TUNNEL DEATH BUILT

CHAPTER 1
DEATH RINGS THE DOORBELL

KERRIGAN, MURDOCH and Klaw very seldom got a chance to spend any time in the comfortable little flat they rented in a quiet section of Washington, not far from the Department of Justice Building. In the last year or so they hadn't slept there more than ten or fifteen times.

Tonight, they were busy making a bookcase for the living-room, when the bell rang. Dan Murdoch was measuring a board for a shelf, while Johnny Kerrigan was sandpapering, and Stephen Klaw was mixing paint.

"I'll take it," said Dan. He closed the roll of metallic measuring tape and went to the door. Significantly, Klaw and Kerrigan both faced the door. Kerrigan put his hand on the heavy revolver in his shoulder holster, and Stephen Klaw's hand went into his trouser pocket. One thing was certain—these three would never be caught napping. The Suicide Squad had too many enemies ever to become careless.

Dan Murdoch opened the door, standing a little to one side. He didn't open it carefully and slowly. Instead, he pulled it wide open with a single sweep.

And then, all three of them gasped. The two people who were

108

An officer shouted a command in a foreign
tongue. The sailors raised their rifles!

standing out there in the hall gave no evidence of menace to
anyone. They were a woman and a girl. The woman was a prim,
efficient-looking lady, attired in a neat tan suit. Upon the lapel

of her jacket there was pinned a large button which read, "Travelers' Aid Society."

The girl had two long braids of deep black hair, which framed rosy cheeks. She was carrying a small overnight bag, and her large, dark, wide eyes were inquisitive and wondering as she looked from one to the other of the three men. She was about eight years old. She was wearing a tan sports coat. Tied by a red string to the top buttonhole of the coat was a large tag, which resembled a railway express tag.

"Er—haven't you made a mistake, madam?" Dan Murdoch stammered. "Were you looking for—"

"Mr. John F. Kerrigan!" the Travelers' Aid lady said primly. "That is one of the three names under the door bell."

"Ah, yes, of course. Mr. Kerrigan!" Dan turned and nodded toward Johnny. "Here is Mr. Kerrigan, madam."

Johnny put down the sandpaper. He came to the door, looking puzzled.

"Yes?" he asked.

The little girl looked up at him and smiled. The Travelers' Aid lady regarded his shirt sleeves with disapproval.

"Mr. Kerrigan, this little girl just arrived on the nine o'clock train from Houston, Texas. She has been consigned to you."

Johnny Kerrigan had been good-naturedly returning the girl's smile. Now the smile froze on his face.

"Did you say—*consigned* to me?"

"Exactly!"

The prim lady reached over and fingered the tag tied to the little girl's coat.

"See for yourself!"

Johnny bent clown and read the tag:

"Travelers' Aid:

Please see that this young lady reaches the home of Mr. John F. Kerrigan, at 1014 Blank Street, Washington, D.C. Thank you."

Johnny looked bewildered. "Well, I'll he damned!"

"*Please!*" The Travelers' Aid lady frowned. "*Such* language! Remember, young man—there are ladies present!"

"I'm sorry!" Johnny exclaimed. "But—I don't understand—" THE LITTLE girl's eyes suddenly filled with tears. "Don't you *want* me, Uncle Johnny? Aunt Martha said you'd be glad to take care of me."

"Now don't cry!" Johnny said hastily. He stepped forward and put a hand on the little girl's soft, dark hair, "Come right in, and we'll see what this is all about."

"Just a minute, young man!" the Travelers' Aid lady said suspiciously. "It appears there has been a mistake. You don't know this girl?"

"Well, no—"

"And you don't know any Aunt Martha?"

"No—"

"Then she's a stranger to you?"

"I'm afraid so."

"In that case, I shall have to take her to the YWCA. I *thought* there was something queer about the whole thing!"

"Queer?" Johnny asked.

"Exactly." The Travelers' Aid lady arched her eyebrows. "This little girl has refused to give me her name!"

"Ah!" said Johnny Kerrigan. He looked at Klaw and Murdoch, who were watching interestedly. Then he swung back to the visitors. "Come in, please. Let's talk this over."

"It will not be necessary," said the Travelers' Aid lady. "I see now, that some mistake must have been made. Whoever sent this little girl on the long train ride from Texas shall be prosecuted—"

"Just a minute," Johnny interrupted. He looked down at the little girl, and smiled. "Is it a secret—about your name?"

She nodded, very seriously. "Aunt Martha made me promise I'd not tell my name to anyone but you. She—she gave me a letter for you. Here it is."

From inside her coat she brought out a sealed envelope which she handed to Johnny. "Aunt Martha said that you would surely keep the bad men from hurting me."

"You bet we will!" Johnny said. There was a sudden gleam of interest in his eyes. And that gleam was reflected in the optics of Dan Murdoch and Stephen Klaw as they both crowded around the Travelers' Aid lady and fairly carried her into the room.

Johnny put his arm around the little girl's shoulders, and led her inside, too. Steve Klaw left the elderly lady to Murdoch, and closed the door, and locked it. Then, without a word, he faded into the next room, which was dark, and went to the window. He pulled the shade aside an inch. Carefully, he scanned both sides of the street, noting each passer-by, and inspecting each car. His gaze fastened on one automobile which was just pulling up at the opposite curb. It was a large car, of the type which is generally used to follow hearses in funerals. It was full of men, and Steve could see the glowing tips of several cigarettes. Half a dozen men climbed out of it and stood staring at the house occupied by the Suicide Squad. They whispered among themselves for a moment, then started across.

Stephen Klaw smiled tightly in the darkness, and let the shade fall back into place. He returned to the living room.

Johnny Kerrigan had the letter open, but he had not started to read it yet. The Travelers' Aid lady was saying, "My name is Miss Dean—Abigail Dean. I am in charge of the Travelers' Aid depot at the Union Station. It is our task to take care of such waifs as this little girl. Each year, hundreds of children are sent by train without escort—"

"Of course, Miss Dean," Dan Murdoch interrupted suavely. "We are sure that your work is very praiseworthy indeed. Can you tell us if you think you were followed from the station?"

Miss Abigail Dean looked startled. "Followed? Why in the world—"

Both Johnny and Dan looked inquiringly at Stephen Klaw. Steve nodded solemnly.

"Ah!" said Dan Murdoch. He went over to the desk near the window, opened the drawer and took out a pair of shoulder holsters. He strapped these on, and put on his coat, over them. Johnny Kerrigan went into the next room and came back in a moment wearing his own coat and carrying Stephen Klaw's.

"There are five or six of them," he murmured to Johnny.

The little girl was watching them, wide-eyed. Abigail Dean

looked shocked and alarmed. "Look here, young men, I don't understand what is going on here, and I don't like it—"

But none of them was paying her any attention. Dan Murdoch and Stephen Klaw were peering over Johnny's shoulder, reading the letter which the girl had given him:

"Dear Mr. Kerrigan:

I am taking the liberty of sending little Nora Dixon to you, and placing her under your protection. God help me, I don't know where else to turn. Do you remember Rod Dixon? He was your friend. He went to college with you, and after he was graduated, became a pursuit pilot in China, where he was killed. Nora is his sister. I am their aunt. Rod once told me that if ever danger threatened Nora, you were the one to help her. Nora had inherited immense properties in New York, under the will of her grandfather. And there is a man in New York who will take any step to prevent Nora's claiming her inheritance. That man's name is Nicodemus Largo. He is wealthy and powerful, and he means to kill her. His men are coming for Nora, and I must send her away from here, before they come. Take her to New York. Protect her. See an attorney there by the name of Pierre Delameter. He will explain all. Be on guard every second of the day and night, for Nicodemus Largo is an evil and dangerous man, cunning and ruthless. God bless you. And thank you for what you may do for Nora.

Martha Dixon."

SLOWLY, JOHNNY Kerrigan folded the letter and thrust it into his pocket. He frowned. "Nicodemus Largo, eh!"

"A nice name," Stephen Klaw said drily. "I think I'll enjoy meeting the gentleman!"

Johnny turned to the little girl. She was watching him breathlessly, holding the hand of Miss Abigail Dean. Johnny studied her. "So," he said softly. So you're Rod Dixon's little sister!"

She nodded eagerly. "Aunt Martha said you were Rod's best friend. She said you'd not let anyone hurt me—"

Johnny strode over to her, and lifted her from the chair in his arms. He pressed her close to him.

"No one is going to hurt you, Nora—ever!" he murmured.

Miss Abigail Dean arose stiffly. "If you will be good enough to explain to me, young man—"

Abruptly, the doorbell rang with a sudden, jarring clamor. Johnny looked at Stephen Klaw. "Did you say there were six of then, Shrimp?"

Steve nodded.

Dan Murdoch grinned. "Nice odds—"

"Nix," said Stephen Klaw. "There's Miss Dean and Nora."

"So?" Johnny asked.

"So—we call the cops."

The doorbell rang again, this time more insistently.

Johnny Kerrigan shrugged. "I guess you're right, Shrimp." He jerked his head toward the phone. "Go ahead, Dan."

Dan Murdoch's long legs brought him to the phone in an instant. But it was with very evident distaste that he picked up the instrument. Never before had the Suicide Squad asked for outside help.

The doorbell continued to ring as Dan jiggled the hook, with the receiver at his ear. The others watched him tensely. Slowly, a smile spread across his features. He replaced the receiver on the hook. "The wire is cut," he said. And he sounded as if he liked it. Stephen Klaw and Johnny Kerrigan were grinning, too.

Steve Klaw took Miss Abigail Dean by the elbow. "If you don't mind, would you step into the next room for a few minutes?"

"But—but—what's going to happen? Why are you all wearing guns? Who is ringing the doorbell? I don't like this—"

"Neither do we, Miss Dean," Steve said with a grin. He led her into the bedroom, and Kerrigan followed with Nora in his arms.

"Now just keep the door closed," Steve told them. "And if you should hear sounds like the backfire of automobiles, pay no attention to them."

Little Nora Dixon looked up trustingly at Johnny Kerrigan. "I'm hungry, Uncle Johnny," she said.

He smiled. "We'll get you a big steak—"

"I don't like steak. I like hot dogs—"

"Hot dogs it'll be, then. And chocolate layer cake, and strawberries and ice cream!"

"My lands!" exclaimed Miss Abigail Dean. "Do you want to ruin the little girl's stomach? I certainly won't leave her with you, if that's the way you're going to feed her. Why, you'll kill the child—"

Johnny and Steve were already out of the room. Steve winked at Abigail. "See you soon, Miss Dean. Better go over in that corner with Nora. Stay out of line with the door."

He closed the door, and turned around. Johnny Kerrigan

had already taken up a position in front of the hall door. Dan Murdoch had faded back into the darkness of the hallway at the left, which led to the other bedrooms. He was out of sight. The doorbell was ringing harder than ever.

Stephen Klaw hurried around the room, putting out all the lights save for a dim one over the desk. Then he moved over behind the unfinished bookcase and crouched down low, both hands in his coat pockets. "All set, Johnny!" he called.

CHAPTER 2
MEET MR. MONK

JOHNNY KERRIGAN nodded, and stepped close to the door. "Who is it?" he called. The bell stopped ringing at once. There was a pause, and then a smooth voice said:

"Mr. Kerrigan? Mr. John F. Kerrigan?"

"That's right."

"May I come in?"

"Who are you?"

"You wouldn't know me, Mr. Kerrigan. My name is Monk. Homer Monk. I'd like to talk to you on business."

Johnny grinned. "What kind of business. Mr. Monk?"

"Well, something that may be profitable to you. You will be wise to open the door."

"I'm not interested," said Johnny. "If you're a canvasser, you're wasting your time."

"I assure you I'm not a canvasser, Mr. Kerrigan. I want to see you on business. Won't you open the door? It's so hard to talk this way."

"Well, all right," Johnny said, as if he were making a grudging concession. He turned the catch, and pulled the door open.

A compact group of men swept into the room. There were six of them in all. Their leader was nattily dressed. He wore a black homburg, set at a jaunty angle, a dark topcoat, suede gloves and spats. Altogether, he gave the impression of a wealthy man-about-town. But his lips were just a little too thin, and his eyes a little too close together.

He waved his gloved hand casually, and one of his followers closed the hall door and stood in front of it, a hand dug deep into his coat pocket. The others fanned out around the room. Each kept his eyes on Johnny Kerrigan; each had his hands in his pockets.

The leader bowed to Johnny. "I am Homer Monk, Mr. Kerrigan. Forgive me if I do not find it necessary to introduce my friends."

"Tell your friends to get the hell out of here," Johnny said. "I didn't invite a whole covey of rats in here."

Mr. Monk raised a gloved hand "Tut, tut," he said deprecatingly. "You must not insult my friends. They are very touchy. They might resent it. I am afraid they must remain—till we have finished our business."

"What's your business?" Kerrigan asked uncompromisingly.

Mr. Homer Monk moved a little closer.

"The girl, Mr. Kerrigan," he said very softly. "I want the girl."

"What girl?"

Mr. Monk made an impatient gesture. "Let's not beat around the bush. A certain girl came here from Houston, Texas, within the hour. She arrived on the nine o'clock train, with a tag tied to her coat. That tag was addressed to you."

"How do you know all that?" Johnny asked.

Mr. Monk shrugged. "Our agents got to Houston just after the girl's aunt had sent her out of town. They found out all about the tag and phoned me in New York. We flew down tonight. We missed Nora Dixon's train, but the Travelers' Aid Bureau at the station told us the rest."

Monk spread his hands, and smiled, "So you see, Mr. Kerrigan, we know Nora Dixon is here. It's no use your denying it."

"So what?" Johnny asked tightly.

"So you will turn her over to us."

"Why?"

Monk raised his eyebrows. "This is why."

From an inside pocket he took a legal looking document. He unfolded it, and thrust it at Johnny Kerrigan.

"Read!"

Johnny took the paper. He glanced around at the five men who had accompanied Monk into the room. They were spread out in a sort of circle, watching him tensely. Their faces were grim and hard.

JOHNNY DROPPED his eyes to the document. His lips tightened as he read. It was a court order, appointing Nicodemus Largo the lawful guardian of Nora Dixon. It authorized him to send for her, and to see that she was brought to New York.

Kerrigan read it over swiftly, then looked up at Monk.

"You're not Nicodemus Largo," he said.

"No. But I am Mr. Largo's legal representative. I am the proprietor of the Homer Monk Detective Agency, in New York, and these men are my operatives. Mr. Nicodemus Largo has hired us to find the Dixon girl, and bring her to New York."

"Are you sure," Johnny asked slowly, "that Nicodemus Largo hasn't hired you to find Nora Dixon—*and kill her?*"

Monk's face became suddenly white and taut. "So! The girl's aunt has been giving you a story, eh?" He tried to talk casually, but Johnny could see that his question had struck home.

"Yes," he said, "Martha Dixon has given me a story. Till I find out what's behind it, I'm not letting Nora Dixon out of my care."

Monk studied him carefully. "Mr. Kerrigan, you're a fool. I don't know what business you're in, but you must have a little common sense. Let me tell you that no one—*no one*—has ever dared to buck Nicodemus Largo. If you try it, he'll wreck you. If you're in business for yourself, he'll send you into bankruptcy. If you're employed, he'll bring pressure on your employer to fire you. He'll hound you for the rest of your life."

Johnny laughed harshly. He held out the court order in front of Monk's face. Then he deliberately proceeded to tear it into pieces. When he finished, he dropped the pieces at Monk's feet.

"Now get the hell out of here!" he said.

Homer Monk's eyes became as small as gimlet holes.

"So!" he purred. "You want it the hard way!"

He raised one of his gloved hands in signal, and spoke swift, clipped orders to his men.

"Belek! Riker! Handle him. As little noise as possible. Pinto, Schwinn, Ebers! Go through the apartment. Find the girl!"

Guns appeared in the hands of all five. Two of them closed in swiftly on Johnny, while the others moved over toward the bedroom door. Homer Monk produced a small black pistol and pointed it at Johnny.

"If you think I'd hesitate to plug you through the heart, you're crazy. You're resisting a court order."

For the moment, none of them was facing toward the unfinished bookcase. So none of them saw the slim, wiry figure of Stephen Klaw. He stepped out from behind the bookcase, with an automatic in each hand. The snick of the two safety catches as he flicked them off sounded loud in the sudden quietness of the room.

"Tch, tch," he said. "Such bad manners. Are these friends of yours, Mr. Kerrigan?"

Homer Monk and his five gunmen jumped as if they had been pricked with needles.

During the momentary diversion, Johnny Kerrigan deftly produced his own revolvers. He chuckled.

"Friends of mine, Mr. Klaw? I'm surprised at you, Mr. Klaw."

"Excuse it please, Mr. Kerrigan," said Steve.

Homer Monk barked, "Take them, men. There's only two—"

Once more he was interrupted, this time from the direction of the hallway which led to the other rooms.

It was Dan Murdoch's voice which intruded courteously upon him.

"A slight mistake, my dear sir. There are *three* of us!"

Murdoch was standing in the archway, with two guns in his hands, and smiling pleasantly.

The sudden appearance of these armed reinforcements—plus the two guns which Johnny Kerrigan had produced—appeared to have a shocking effect upon these gunmen. They had apparently expected to have to deal with one, unarmed man. It was quite evident that they were not aware of the real identity of these three.

THERE HAD been a good deal in the papers about Kerrigan and Murdoch and Klaw. But always in that order, and always without Christian names. And though much had been written about the exploits of the Suicide Squad, Kerrigan and Murdoch and Klaw had never permitted much to be written about them individually. In fact, the F.B.I. never encouraged agents to give out publicity about themselves, and these three hellions didn't care about publicity anyway. Rather, they shunned it. All that was known about them was that they were never sent out on a routine case, but were always kept in reserve for those assignments which were so dangerous that the director hesitated even to ask for volunteers. They got those jobs from which there was little chance of returning alive.

Originally, there had been five of them. Then there were only four. Now there were three—Kerrigan and Murdoch and Klaw. They lived from day to day, and took what life brought them. Tomorrow, they might have an appointment with death, and then there might be only two, or one, or none. But that was the way they wanted it. They needed the constant presence of Death at their elbows to give zest to their life. In fact, the saying went in the Underworld, that Kerrigan and Murdoch and Klaw pursued the Grim Reaper so relentlessly that he had grown shy of them.

But these gunmen of Homer Monk's—though they had all heard of the Suicide Squad—hadn't connected the names on the door plate with that most dangerous trio.

Johnny Kerrigan's eyes crinkled with laughter as he watched the bewildered expression on Homer Monk's face.

"You see," he explained, "my friends and I have arranged a very nice reception for you. Permit me to introduce them—Murdoch and Klaw. As you see, they are prepared to offer you very effective entertainment."

The gunmen stared around the room at the three, in evident indecision. They were waiting for word from Homer Monk.

But suddenly, as they stood there, one of the gunmen uttered a startled exclamation. "Kerrigan! And Murdoch and Klaw!" He turned a white face to Homer Monk. "Boss! It's the *Suicide Squad!* We've come up against the whole damned *Suicide Squad!*"

Before any of them could digest the information, Stephen Klaw moved forward, his guns at his hips. He glanced at Kerrigan, and then at Murdoch. "What say, mopes?"

Dan Murdoch nodded, from his position in the archway. "You take it from here, Shrimp."

Klaw nodded. He smiled benignly at one after the other of the six gunmen.

"Now gentlemen," he said mildly, "let's get down to business. You all have guns in your hands. You can start shooting right now—or you can gently put your guns down on the floor. It's all the same to us."

123

The gunman who had just recognized their names was the first to weaken.

"Pass me!" he said, and bent down and very carefully laid his gun on the floor. Then he straightened and raised his hands above his head.

"Thank you," Stephen Klaw said sardonically. "And now—anybody else? Or do the rest of you want to shoot it out?"

ONE AFTER the other, the remaining gunmen followed the example of the first, until the only one left holding a gun was Homer Monk. Monk glared from one to the other of his followers, his lips curled with scorn. "You yellow rats!" he spat out. "What do you get paid for? Wait'll the big boss hears about this!"

He glared at the one who had first laid down his weapon. "You, Ebers! Why didn't you keep your mouth shut? There are six of us. We could have shot them down. They're only human. You had to go and turn yellow. You'll hear more about this—"

Ebers shrugged. "I only got one life to lose, boss, and I'm not anxious to lose it right now. These three guys are plenty tough, and they play for keeps. Me, I'd rather not swap lead with them!"

Monk's dark face twitched spasmodically. He hesitated for a fraction of a second. Then he lowered his black pistol and bent down. He laid it on the floor with the other weapons.

"Thank you so much," Stephen Klaw said. He nodded toward the hall door. "That's the way out."

Johnny Kerrigan grinned. He holstered his guns, stepped to the door, and pulled it open. "This way, gentlemen!"

Monk hesitated. "Our guns—"

"We'll save them for you," Johnny grinned.

One by one, the defeated gunmen filed out of the room. Ebers winked weakly at Johnny as he filed past. The others were sullen, and glowering.

Homer Monk was the last to leave. As he stepped out into the corridor, he turned and faced Kerrigan. His small, close-set eyes were burning. His fists were clenched.

"Would you care for a little advice, my friends?" he said softly. "Don't come to New York. Don't bring the Dixon girl to claim her inheritance. You won the first round, because I didn't know what I was coming up against. But in New York it'll be different. Don't think that because you're G-men, and because you're tough, you have a chance against Nicodemus Largo. He has vast resources—and plenty of pull. He'll break you—the three of you. Within five minutes, I'll be talking to him on the long distance. In ten minutes, he'll be burning up the phones. By tomorrow morning you won't be G-men any more. And—if you come to New York—by tomorrow night you won't be alive any more!"

"Thank you," said Stephen Klaw, coming to the door beside Johnny Kerrigan. "Thank you for everything. And when you talk to Nicodemus Largo—tell him that we'll be in New York in the morning!"

CHAPTER 3
PAGING MR. DANGER

MISS ABIGAIL DEAN came stalking out of the bedroom as soon as the door had closed behind Monk and his men. She had Nora by the hand, and her prim face was set in determined lines.

"I declare!" she exclaimed. "This is all utterly incredible. I heard every word of what went on. Those wicked gangsters should be boiled in oil. Why didn't you boys pump them full of lead?"

Kerrigan, Murdoch and Klaw stared at her.

"Why my dear Miss Dean!" said Dan Murdoch. "Such language! I never thought you were so bloodthirsty!"

Abigail Dean put her arm around little Nora Dixon, and pressed her close.

"It's outrageous!" she barked. "Such things shouldn't be permitted. I could tell from the voice of that man Monk that he's a vicious criminal. If you three boys are really G-men, why didn't you arrest them?"

By common consent, Kerrigan and Klaw left it to Murdoch to explain things to her. Murdoch, with his dark eyes and dark hair, his slender litheness and his soft-spoken manner, was the ideal diplomat for the ladies.

"They had a court order, Miss Dean," he said. "We really have nothing on them. There's no proof that they wanted to harm Nora. If we arrested them, they'd be out in half an hour."

"But what about the letter from Aunt Martha Dixon? *She* says they plan to—to stop Nora from going to New York—"

"Unfortunately," Dan told her, "Aunt Martha's letter is no proof. It's only a suspicion. It wouldn't stand up in court."

Abigail Dean pressed Nora closer to her breast. "You poor little thing!" she crooned. "Don't be frightened."

Nora crinkled her nose, looked at Dan Murdoch, then at Kerrigan and Klaw, and smiled. "I'm not frightened. Aunt Martha said Uncle Johnny wouldn't let anything happen to me. And now I have three uncles. They'll scare the bad men away."

"You bet we will!" Murdoch smiled.

"I'm hungry," said Nora.

Kerrigan nodded. "I'll go down and get some grub. Hot dogs, pickles, olives, a can of spaghetti and a can of corn, chocolate layer cake and soda pop!" He stroked Nora's hair. "How's that for supper?"

Nora's eyes were sparkling. "Ooh! And can we have some whipped cream for the cake?"

"Sure. We'll do it right—"

"You'll do nothing of the kind, young man!" Miss Abigail Dean said sternly. She sniffed. "Pickles! Spaghetti! Hot dogs! Soda pop!"

With the air of a crusader, she strode across the room to the desk and snatched up paper and pencil. "Here! This is what you'll get. Lamb chops, a can of green peas—"

She wrote out the list and handed it to Johnny. "A lot *you* know about feeding children!"

Kerrigan had an abashed look as he took the paper. Miss Dean scowled at him. "And no soda pop, either. You get a container of milk!"

"Yes, ma'am!" Johnny said meekly.

HE TURNED around to get his hat, and saw Klaw and Murdoch grinning at him. Klaw got his hat, too, and Kerrigan said, "Where are *you* going, Shrimp?"

"To get four reservations on the New York plane. We're not waiting for morning. We're leaving tonight—the four of us—"

"The *five* of us!" Miss Abigail Dean corrected. "You make that *five* tickets, young man." She glared at Steve. "You don't think I'd let Nora go to New York with you three lummoxes to care for her, do you? My lands! You don't know the first thing about looking after a child—"

"But look here, Miss Dean," Murdoch protested. "You don't have to go to all that trouble—"

"You can save your breath, young man! I've made up my mind. It's my job to see that this child is placed in competent hands. And I'm going to stay with her till I'm satisfied that she'll be fed and cared for properly!"

Murdoch looked helplessly at Stephen Klaw.

Klaw studied Abigail Dean for a moment. "You heard what happened here just now, Miss Dean. You realize it may be dangerous—"

"I do. All the more reason for me to go along!"

Suddenly, Stephen Klaw smiled, "We'll be glad to have you, Miss Dean!"

"Thank you." She sniffed. "And don't call me Miss Dean. Call me Abby."

Just then the doorbell rang.

Abby clutched Nora more tightly, her face going white. "It's those terrible men again—"

Stephen Klaw went to the door. Kerrigan and Murdoch drew their guns and flanked him, grimly.

"Open it!" Kerrigan ordered.

Steve turned the latch and pulled the door open.

A Western Union messenger was standing outside. He almost jumped out of his skin when he glimpsed the guns pointed at him.

"Sorry," Klaw said with a grin. "Pay no attention to my two friends. They're practicing for the movies. What is it?"

The boy held out a telegram in a trembling hand. "M-mister Klaw?"

Steve took the telegram, signed for it, and gave the boy a half dollar. As soon as the door was closed, he ripped the envelope open, with Kerrigan and Murdoch peering over his shoulder.

The message was from their Chief, the Director of the Federal Bureau of Investigation:

STEPHEN KLAW
MERRIMAC APARTMENTS
WHAT IS TROUBLE WITH YOUR PHONE? HAVE BEEN TRYING TO GET YOU FOR TEN MINUTES REPORT AT ONCE WITH KERRIGAN AND MURDOCH. HAVE IMPORTANT ASSIGNMENT FOR YOU.

"Nuts!" said Johnny. "Just when we have a little private business of our own! I figured we'd get a furlough—"

Stephen Klaw thrust the telegram in his pocket. "I'll go over and see the Chief." He turned to Murdoch. "Think you can keep control here, in case those bozos try a come-back?"

Murdoch merely grinned.

AT THE Department of Justice Building, a light was burning in the Director's office, though it was almost ten o'clock in the evening. There were many other lights burning in that building, too, as well as in dozens of other government bureaus throughout Washington. The nation's capital was working on twenty-four-hour shifts these days, on the tremendous task of integrating our huge resources into unified National Defense.

Steve didn't have to wait. He was immediately admitted to the director's private office.

"Where are Kerrigan and Murdoch?" the Chief demanded. "I've got to talk to all three of you together. The job I have for you is dangerous—and tricky. And you have to get started at once!"

Steve sat down. "You—er—couldn't get anyone else to handle it, sir, could you?"

The director looked at Steve, and frowned. "I'm afraid not, Steve. This is the kind of thing you three are always looking for. I'd never assign any of my regular men to it, because it's like sending them into a death trap. What's the matter with you, Steve? Don't you want the assignment?"

Klaw sighed. "We thought we'd ask for a furlough for a couple of days. There's a little girl—the sister of a fellow who was a friend of Johnny's. She's in trouble, and we'd like to help her."

The Director looked disappointed. "I was counting on you three—"

"Couldn't we split up, sir?" Steve asked hopefully. "Suppose one of us were to take care of your assignment, and the other two handled the little girl's case—"

"This job," the director said grimly, "will take everything all three of you can put into it. The man we're after is a clever and insidious criminal—on a huge scale. I suppose you've read the confidential reports about the theft, three months ago, of twenty thousand of the new-type semi-automatic rifles?"

"Yes, sir. They were stolen from the factory by a small army of thugs. They mowed down the guards and truckmen with machine guns, then drove the whole convoy away. The rifles were never found."

"Right. Well, do you know that five thousand of those rifles were sold to a certain South American republic, where a revolution was attempted? If we hadn't been able to get two of our destroyers to that country at a moment's notice, the revolution would have succeeded!"

"I see!" said Steve.

"Furthermore, there have been mysterious agents in other South American countries, offering the rest of these automatic rifles for sale. Those rifles are so efficient and so deadly that a force of five thousand revolutionists equipped with them could defeat an army ten times their numbers."

"And you want Kerrigan and Murdoch and me to recover those rifles, sir?"

"Exactly. We have received secret information from G-2 that the bulk of those stolen rifles are to be shipped out of the country tomorrow, and delivered to a country in Central America, within flying distance of the Panama Canal. If those rifles are delivered, and if a revolution takes place, the Canal will be seriously threatened. Those rifles must be prevented from leaving the country. All we know is the name of the man who is suspected of having engineered the theft, and who is selling them to South America.

He controls the organization which stole them, and which is distributing them. But there is not one jot of proof against him. This is a job that requires fast, unconventional work. So far, the theft of the rifles has not been made public. But tomorrow, in the House of Representatives, a certain Congressman is going to demand a public investigation. Can you imagine the scandal and the loss of morale to our National Defense plans, if that information becomes known? The only way to counteract it is to be able to announce that the stolen rifles have been recovered. *That's your job!*"

Steve shifted, uncomfortably in his chair. "But this little girl, Nora—"

The Director hurried on, as if he hadn't heard. "The man we suspect controls a huge amount of wealth. He has used it to make himself impregnable. His ruthlessness makes him the most dangerous man in America. Yes, I can say that Nicodemus Largo is the greatest threat to American security within this country—"

Stephen Klaw sat up straight in the chair. "Sir! Did you say *Nicodemus Largo?*"

The Director nodded. "That's his name. He was only a struggling attorney a few years ago, but he was appointed executor of an immense estate, and he started to milk it, using the funds to build up his criminal organization. I had really hoped you'd undertake the job. In fact, I was so certain you'd do it, that I've already ordered three tickets on the night plane for New York—"

Steve's eyes were glittering. "Make it *five* tickets, sir. We'll leave at once!"

CHAPTER 4
DEATH DRIVES CROSSTOWN

T HE ELECTRIC clock in the all-night restaurant on Fifth Avenue showed ten minutes after three. The restaurant was quiet, almost deserted save for two night-hawk cab drivers whose taxis were parked outside in the bitter cold. Their heads were close together as they pored over a racing form, and they paid no attention to Stephen Klaw, who sat at a window table, drinking his third cup of black coffee.

Fifth Avenue was slumbering. Only an occasional car flashed by.

Steve sipped his coffee slowly. Looking through the plate-glass window, he could see the glowing tip of Johnny Kerrigan's cigarette in a doorway, directly across the street.

He glanced up at the clock. The minute hand moved ponderously down another notch. Three-eleven.

A cab pulled up at the curb, and a man descended from it. He was in his fifties, with a small gray moustache and a pair of gold-rimmed glasses. Steve watched him as he spoke to the cab driver, apparently telling him to wait. Then he turned, looked furtively behind him, and hurried into the restaurant. He stopped, just inside, the warm breath blowing from his lips, and looked uncertainly at Stephen Klaw.

Klaw nodded to him, and arose. "Right here, Mr. Delameter," he said.

The gray-moustached man threw another frightened glance

133

behind him, then came over to the table. He slipped into the chair Steve held for him. He seemed almost terrified.

"Mr. Klaw? Mr. Stephen Klaw?" he asked jerkily.

"That's right," said Steve. "You came promptly."

"I dressed as quickly as possible after you phoned, and came right over. But—but I've been followed!"

"Ah!" said Steve.

"But never mind about me," Delameter hurried on hastily. "Tell me about Nora Dixon. Is—is she safe?"

"She is."

"She's here—in New York?"

"Yes."

"Where?"

Steve smiled tightly. "Let's just leave it at that for the time being—till I've talked to you a little more. Just take my word for it that she's well protected. Now, what about your being followed?"

Pierre Delameter nodded. "They watch me day and night. Every move I make is known. There—" he jerked his head toward the street—"that car pulling up behind my cab. The two men in it were outside my house when I left."

"I see," said Stephen Klaw, watching the two men who emerged from the car. It was the same kind of car which Homer Monk had used last night, in Washington—a seven passenger limousine. Steve's eyes narrowed. He recognized the two men. They were two of the gunmen who had been with Monk last night.

They peered in through the plate glass window, saw Klaw and Delameter, and immediately started to come inside.

"You see!" exclaimed Delameter. "They just play with me, the way a cat plays with a mouse. I wonder that they haven't killed me before now. Maybe they will tonight—"

"Buck up," said Steve. "You can only get killed once."

"I'm not afraid for myself," the other said slowly. "It's little Nora Dixon that I'm worried about. If anything should happen to me, there'd be no one to protect her. Nicodemus Largo could do whatever he wanted with her."

"Not exactly," Steve told him grimly. "Nora has three new uncles who are looking after her."

The two gunmen were in the restaurant now. They threw searching glances at Steve and Delameter, and Steve returned the stares, grinning just a little. He had one hand in his coat pocket, but otherwise he seemed to be entirely at ease. The two men did not return his grin. Instead, they looked quickly away, though he was certain that they recognized him. They selected a table near the wall, behind Steve.

KLAW WINKED at Delameter, and moved his chair around so that he was facing them again. He kept his eyes on them, and talked to Delameter. "Nora's aunt said that you would tell us all about this business."

"Yes, of course. As you know, I'm an attorney. I was close friend of Nora's grandfather, Horace Dixon."

"Then how was it," Steve demanded, "that he named Nicodemus Largo as executor of his estate, and not you?"

"Because I was in South America at the time. Horace wrote to me, telling me that he was naming Largo as executor, but at the same time he said that he would provide in his will that Largo must make an annual accounting, which must be approved by me. And further, the will provides that when Nora is nine years old, I am to be appointed guardian, and Largo is to turn the estate over to me to manage until Nora reaches her eighteenth birthday—"

"But we saw a court order," Steve interrupted, "in which Nicodemus Largo is appointed guardian—"

"Exactly! Largo has used his immense power and influence to have the will modified, so that he can become guardian. In that way, he will not have to turn the property over, and can continue to use it for his own advantage. I have spent months and months compiling figures, and I can prove that Nicodemus Largo has diverted from the estate at least two million dollars during the last five years.

"Then why not prosecute him?"

Delameter smiled wryly. "I wouldn't live over night. And I'd get nowhere, bucking his power and influence. I could show you papers—"

"Where are these papers? At your office?"

The older man shook his head bleakly. "My home and my office have been ransacked on a dozen different occasions. I have those papers in another place, and I don't dare go near them, for fear that Nicodemus Largo will discover where they are."

"Take me there!" said Stephen Klaw.

"No! No! Are you mad? Those two men—they'll follow us—"

"They won't follow us tonight," Klaw said grimly.

"How—how will you stop them?"

"Watch."

Elaborately, Steve lit a cigarette. Then he glanced through the plate glass window toward the spot where Johnny Kerrigan was standing.

"Let's go," he said.

He called the waiter over, paid the check, and got up without looking at the two men at the other table. Then he took Delameter's arm and led him toward the door.

"Where is this secret place of yours?"

"Near the East River. Twenty-fifth Street."

"Okay."

They pushed out through the revolving doors.

The two men had already left their table, and were coming out after them, quickly.

As Steve and the attorney reached the sidewalk, Johnny Kerrigan got there from across the street. Johnny gave no sign of recognition, and neither did Steve. But as they brushed past each other, Steve whispered swiftly, "Discourage the two muggs, Johnny. I'm heading for the East River and Twenty-fifth Street."

"Right!" said Johnny Kerrigan.

Steve led Delameter to the waiting cab, and pushed him in.

Delameter looked bewildered. "I don't understand—"

He glanced backward, and saw the two muggs standing just outside the restaurant. Johnny Kerrigan was right behind them, and Johnny was whispering in their ears. Also, Johnny was holding two gleaming objects poked into their ribs.

Steve chuckled, and said to the cab driver, "East River and Twenty-fifth Street, pal."

The cab pulled away, leaving Johnny and his two unwilling companions in front of the restaurant.

PIERRE DELAMETER shook his head. "I'm not a man of violence. I'm unused to this kind of thing. Yet—I would almost have liked to see your friend beat the hell out of those two gunmen!"

"It's funny," Steve grinned, "but every respectable person who comes in contact with those birds begins to use the damnedest language."

"I would like to do more than use language on them!" Pierre Delameter said fiercely. "You would understand how I feel, if you could see the people whose lives have been ruined by that vicious organization of Nicodemus Largo. Nora Dixon is only one of hundreds. He forces men and women to do the most criminal things—"

"How does he force them?" Steve asked.

"God knows. He terrorizes them, brings pressure to bear on them through business, or through friends and relatives. He has spies everywhere. He ferrets things out about people—"

"What has he on you?" Steve asked.

Delameter stiffened. He turned a haggard face to Steve.

"What—what do you mean?"

Klaw smiled grimly. "There's another car following us, Delameter. That whole business back there in the restaurant was an act. You deliberately called my attention to those two birds, who were supposed to be following you. The idea was, that

I wouldn't notice the others. So, the conclusion I draw is: after I phoned you and made the appointment, you called Nicodemus Largo, and told him about it. He sent two cars out. One was a blind for the other."

Pierre Delameter's face was white and drawn.

"It's true," he said hoarsely. "God help me, it's true!"

Steve nodded. "You're doing it against your will. Nicodemus Largo has something on you."

"Yes. Yes, he has something on me. I'll tell you—"

"Never mind," Steve said softly. "I don't give a damn what he has on you, or what you've done in the past. It's the present I'm interested in. Where are you taking me now? Into a trap?"

"God help me, yes!" Delameter groaned. "They're going to kill you!"

"So nice of them," said Steve.

"Believe me," Delameter protested, "I would not have done it if I had had any other alternative. I don't know how you managed to guess so much—"

"It's my business," Steve grinned. "It's my business to smell danger. If it weren't for that, I'd have been dead long ago. What about this trap? How is it going to be sprung?"

"This place I'm taking you to—there will be men stationed on the upper floor. I'm to take you in, and leave you in the hall for a moment. As soon as I step out of the hall, they'll take over. If you try to retreat those men who are following us will be there to cut off your escape."

"I see," said Steve.

They were driving south along the waterfront now, and

Delameter motioned with his hand. "You see these blocks of warehouses along the docks? They belong to the estate of Horace Dixon. The estate owns a thousand feet of wharfage, besides warehouses. And all of it is in the hands of Nicodemus Largo. I fought him for five years. But—" the old man's voice broke— "he's too powerful for me. Believe me, Stephen Klaw, I am an honest man. If I tried to lead you into a trap, please believe that I had no choice."

"I believe you," Steve said.

They arrived at Twenty-fifth Street, and the cab driver slowed up and came to a stop. They were opposite a huge, bleak warehouse on the river's edge. Alongside the warehouse, there was a low brick building, which backed on the river. In the open lot in front of the low building there was a great quantity of building material, a crane, and several steel girders, as well as a modern pile-driver.

"Nicodemus Largo is doing some special construction work there," Delameter explained. "It's part of the Dixon estate. But no one knows just what is being done. I've tried to find out—"

"Never mind that now," Klaw said. He glanced through the rear window, and saw that the car which had been following them was pulled up about a hundred feet behind. He turned back to Delameter. "Where is this trap you were leading me into?"

"Over there," Delameter said, pointing to a small tenement house down the side street. "I'm supposed to tell you that my papers are hidden in that house. *They* will do the rest. But—now that you know it's a trap, we'll not go near it—"

"On the contrary," Stephen Klaw said softly. "We will!"

CHAPTER 5
SNAP THE TRAP

THEY GOT out of the cab, and Steve paid the driver. He waited till the cab was gone, then took Delameter by the arm and led him over to the corner.

"We'll wait here," he said.

"What for?"

"A little company."

As they stood at the corner, the car which had followed them doused its lights.

Steve chuckled. "They probably think you're trying to sell me the idea of going into that house."

Delameter groaned. "If they only knew that I'm trying to dissuade you! For God's sake, Klaw, remember that you're only human. You can't walk through a barrage of bullets—"

"I don't think they're going to use bullets."

"That's what they told me."

"Maybe that's what they told *you*. But it's not the way they work."

"What do you mean?"

"Has Nicodemus Largo ever been convicted of a crime?" Steve asked, somewhat irrelevantly.

"Of course not. He's too clever."

"Exactly. He's too clever to commit an unmistakable murder. So is Homer Monk. I have reason to know. I saw Monk operate in Washington last night. We caught him cold—stopped him from taking Nora Dixon away. Yet we had no proof that he intended to harm her. If he'd gotten hold of her, do you think he'd just have shot her, or drowned her?"

"No—"

"Of course not. He'd have managed some sort of 'accident.' That's why I think they'll try something subtle—something that will look like an accident."

Delameter stared at Klaw. "I begin to think you are a worthy match for Nicodemus Largo."

He stopped as a black limousine coasted down the waterfront past the watching car, and halted almost alongside them, at the corner.

"God!" exclaimed Delameter. "That's one of Monk's cars! Lookout!"

"It's all right." Stephen Klaw said, grinning. He gripped the lawyer's arm to quiet him, and glanced into the interior of the limousine.

Johnny Kerrigan was driving it. In the tonneau, handcuffed to each other, were the two men from the Fifth Avenue restaurant.

Delameter's eyes opened wide. But he said nothing.

Steve winked at Johnny. "Nice going, Mope."

Johnny grinned. "I thought I might as well bring these two boys along. They didn't put up much of an argument."

"There are a couple more of the same breed," Steve said, "in that car back there. We ought to get them, too."

"Sold," said Kerrigan.

"Wait here," Steve directed Delameter, and jumped on the running-board. "All set, Johnny."

Kerrigan didn't turn the car around. Instead, he put it in reverse, and gave her the gas. The big limousine sped backward as Johnny's foot pushed all the way down to the floorboard. Too late, the occupants of that other limousine realized Johnny's intention. They had no time to get their own car in motion. They opened both doors, and scrambled out. There were just two of them, and they leaped to the ground and began to run.

At he last minute, just before crashing, Johnny twisted the wheel hard and missed the limousine by a hair. Then he yelled, "Hang on, Shrimp!" and stepped down hard on the brake.

The car jarred to a dead stop.

Stephen Klaw hung on with one hand. In the other he had an automatic. He raised it, and shouted to the two running men: "Stand still, or I'll shoot your legs from under you!"

The two gunmen had been yanking at their shoulder holsters as they ran, but the thing had happened so fast that they had not been able to get their guns out. They were caught flat-footed. They stopped and raised their hands in the air.

Johnny backed the car up a little more, and Steve got off and herded the two men over toward the corner, with Johnny following slowly in the limousine.

Delameter was standing just where Steve had left him. He was staring, speechless.

THE TWO men whom Steve had captured were strangers to him. They were not of the party which had accompanied Monk last night.

"Names, please?" Steve inquired.

They were sullen, but cowed.

"My name is Kovey," said one.

"I'm Link," the other added.

"All right, Messers Kovey and Link," Steve said. "You followed me from the restaurant, and you were watching to see what I'd do. What were you expecting?"

They both glanced at Delameter, but said nothing.

"They were waiting to see you go into that house!" Delameter exclaimed. "They were here to keep you from coming out again!"

Klaw looked at Kovey and Link. "Is that true?"

Kovey glared at Delameter. "Squealing, huh?"

The old lawyer threw his shoulders back. "Yes, squealing. And you can tell Nicodemus Largo that I warned Klaw about the trap. Largo can do whatever he wants to me."

"Don't worry," Steve said dryly. "They won't be telling anybody much."

"Be careful," Delameter warned. "There must be more of Largo's men inside that house. If they see that their plans have gone wrong, they may come out and attack you in the street."

Steve shook his head. "Can't you understand, Delameter, that there isn't going to be any shooting here? That whole block of tenements is condemned for the East River Drive improvements. That house is empty."

The old lawyer looked puzzled. "Then—then what kind of trap could it be—"

"Suppose." Johnny Kerrigan broke in, "that we go inside and see for ourselves?"

As he said it, he winked at Stephen Klaw.

Steve appeared to think it over, and then nodded as if he had reached a decision.

"Good idea, Johnny. We'll go in."

As he said it, he watched the faces of the two prisoners. They stared straight ahead, stoically, but Steve detected a gleam in the eyes of the one who called himself Kovey.

"What do you say, Kovey?" he asked gently. "Shall Kerrigan and I go in there and find out what goes on?"

Kovey sneered. "Do whatever you like. You have nothing on us. You can't arrest us for just being around here. We haven't done a thing."

Stephen Klaw nodded. "You're absolutely right, Mr. Kovey. There are no grounds for arresting you. So we're going to let you go—" he stopped for a second, noting the triumphant gleam in the eyes of both prisoners—*"after* you've gone into that house with us!"

Both Kovey and Link jerked erect. They stared at Klaw with wide, distended eyes. "No! For God's sake, no!" Link exclaimed. "You can't make us go in there!"

"Why should you be so scared?" Johnny Kerrigan asked. "Even if you have men waiting there to attack Klaw and me, they surely won't hurt you two."

"We won't go!" Kovey said flatly. He glared at Delameter. "All right. I'll tell you what's in there. There's a couple of boys on the first floor, with sub-machine guns. They've got the front way and the back way covered. The minute you step in there, they'll cut you down. But you can get in through the cellar—"

"That's what Nicodemus told me!" Pierre Delameter broke in. "He said to take you in through the cellar, and up into the hall!"

"Hm!" said Steve. He stepped close to Kovey. "Do you work for Homer Monk?"

"No."

"For whom do you work?"

"If you must know," Kovey sneered, "we work for Nicodemus Largo himself."

"What do you do for him?"

Kovey shrugged. "We're foremen—in charge of construction. We're doing work along the river front."

"How about those two men we have in the car? They work for Monk, don't they?"

"I wouldn't know."

Steve regarded Kovey thoughtfully. "I wonder if *they* know what's in that house?"

"The chances are they don't," Delameter said. "Largo doesn't trust Monk any too much. He gives him specific jobs to do. But for anything important, he uses his own men. These two—Kovey and Link—are two of his most trusted agents."

"I see," said Steve.

He stepped close to Kovey, and went through his pockets. He took his guns away from him and handed them to Delameter.

"You—you trust me?" the lawyer asked with a quaver in his voice. "You trust me after I tried to lead you into a death trap?"

Steve looked him square in the eyes. "You told me you were an honest man, didn't you?"

"Yes—"

"All right."

THERE WERE tears in the old lawyer's eyes as he gathered the guns. Kerrigan was doing the same for Link, and he also handed Delameter the weapons. They went through the papers in both men's pockets. In Kovey's wallet there was a card showing that he was blasting foreman for the Largo Construction Corporation. Link's papers showed him to be a sandhog superintendent, employed by the same Company.

"Well, it checks," Steve said. He looked at Kerrigan, significantly tapping Kovey's card. "Get the idea, Johnny?"

Kerrigan nodded grimly. "I get it, Steve!"

Delameter looked puzzled. "I don't understand—"

He was interrupted by the sound of the car door opening behind them. They had not paid any attention to the two gunmen whom Johnny had handcuffed to each other in the rear of the car. And those two had taken advantage of it. As Johnny and Steve swung around, they saw the door on the far side of the car swinging open, and the two men darting out, unshackled.

"Hell!" exclaimed Johnny. "I cuffed them with their own bracelets, and took the key. They must have had a duplicate!"

He drew his revolver and yelled, "Hey! Hold it!"

But the two men doubled around in front of the car, and raced down the side street, dodging and weaving.

Stephen Klaw swung his automatic around to keep Kovey and Link covered, while Johnny Kerrigan dropped to one knee, sighting his revolver at arm's length.

"Last chance!" Johnny shouted in his stentorian voice. "Stop or I'll shoot!"

The two men were directly opposite the tenement house which they had been studying. As Johnny shouted, they turned and saw him sighting at them. There seemed to be only one chance for them, and they took it. They dived into the basement areaway of that tenement house, disappearing below the embrasure. Johnny Kerrigan had hesitated to fire, feeling sure that they would stop.

But now he jumped up and yelled, "Don't go in there, you fools—"

There was the sound of breaking glass as the two men smashed a basement window pane. They evidently intended to go through the empty house and escape the back way.

Desperately, Johnny shouted, "Stay out! Stay out—"

His voice was drowned by a terrific explosion which buckled the very sidewalk where they stood. A long streamer of yellow flame lanced out of the basement areaway where those two men had disappeared. Mortar and brick and pieces of timber hailed through the air, catapulted as if from a mighty springboard. Debris showered down upon the whole length of the street. And then, the whole tenement house seemed to buckle outward, and crash down upon itself with a roar like a giant waterfall.

Johnny Kerrigan and Stephen Klaw watched that cataclysm with somber eyes. Kovey and Link stood, licking their lips, fists clenched tightly at their sides. And Pierre Delameter stared with unbelieving horror.

"Those two men," he muttered, "they—they must have been blown to bits!"

STEPHEN KLAW nodded. "There, but for the grace of

God, Delameter, go you and I! Nicodemus Largo was sending you, too, to your death, when he forced you to lure me into the trap. Remember! He told you to take me in through the basement!"

"Yes! But—but who—"

"Who planted the explosive?" Johnny Kerrigan asked. He laughed harshly, and took hold of Kovey and Link, each by an arm. They winced under the powerful grip of his fingers. "Here are the two boys who planted the dynamite in that house. That's why they didn't want to go in with us!"

Delameter's eyes widened. "Now I understand. Kovey—he's a blasting foreman! You guessed that there was dynamite in the house!"

Stephen Klaw nodded. "Monk's men hadn't been let in on the secret. Only Kovey and Link. And Nicodemus Largo knew the kind of trap it was."

"Nuts!" spat Link. "You can't prove anything on us."

"I think we can," Steve said quietly.

Kovey laughed. "No one who works for Nicodemus Largo has ever been convicted, wise guy. We're in the clear. There aren't any fingerprints left in that house, either."

"Maybe not," Steve told him. "But you have to have a license to use dynamite. I suppose you stole it from the construction job over there by the river. If so, we can check—"

He stopped, seeing the triumphant grins on the faces of the two men. He glanced at Kerrigan. "We better get out of here, Johnny. I hear fire-bells."

Kerrigan nodded and climbed into the limousine. Steve herded Kovey and Link into the rear, and got in beside them.

"Can you drive?" he asked Delameter.

The lawyer nodded.

"Okay. Get in that other limousine and follow us."

Within two minutes, they were out of the block, and away from the scene of the tragedy.

Johnny drove north for about a mile, not going too fast, so that Delameter might keep up with them in the other car. Then he turned left and headed west toward Central Park. Klaw was sitting astride one of the folding seats in the rear, facing backward and keeping Kovey and Link covered.

Kovey was impassive, but Link was fidgeting nervously. At last, Link burst out, "You have no evidence against us!"

Steve nodded. "You're right, there!"

Link gained courage. "You can't hold us!"

Steve shook his head. "You're *wrong,* there!"

"We're entitled to a lawyer!"

"Sure you are."

"We want a lawyer. We want to use the phone."

Steve said over his shoulder to Kerrigan, "They want to use the phone, Johnny.

"Sure," said Johnny Kerrigan. "I'll stop at the next drug store."

"You have no right to hold us!" Link snarled.

"Not the slightest," Steve agreed with him calmly. "I think it's a damned shame. You ought to write to your congressman about it. By the way—have you got a congressman? Are you a citizen? Have you got a registration card?"

Link lapsed into sullen silence.

WITH DELAMETER in the other car hugging their tail, Johnny drove through the Sixty-sixth Street transverse across Central Park to the west side, then up a few blocks, and stopped before a modest brownstone house on a side street. Delameter pulled up close behind.

Johnny left Steve with the prisoners, and got out of the car.

It was quiet and dark on the street. Down at the far end there was a lone milk wagon. Johnny climbed the high stoop, and before he could ring the bell, the door opened. A gray-haired woman was revealed.

"Hello, Johnny," she said. "I waited up for you. We heard over the radio about the explosion downtown. We thought you might have had something to do with it. Dan Murdoch has been on tenterhooks." She smiled. "He's sore because he had to stay here and guard little Nora, and missed the excitement of battle."

This was Mother Kelly, known wherever F.B.I. agents gathered. Her husband and her son had belonged to the Service, said both had died in the performance of their duty. It was Kerrigan and Murdoch and Klaw who had avenged her son's death. And Mother Kelly supported herself now, by running this exclusive rooming house, catering only to F.B.I. men. She was always ready to help G-men especially Kerrigan, Murdoch and Klaw. Right now, little Nora Dixon and Miss Abigail Dean were sleeping in a room upstairs, with Dan Murdoch guarding the door. And there was no safer place for them in the City of New York!

Johnny Kerrigan patted her shoulder. "We have a couple

of guests we'd like to leave with you, Mother Kelly," he said. "They—er—won't be paying guests."

Mother Kelly raised her eyebrows. "Up in the attic," she said. "We'll give them the Green Room—the one with the padlock on the door!"

Johnny nodded, and returned to the car. He took out his revolver, and nodded to Klaw. Steve smiled very pleasantly at Kovey and Link.

"All right, gentlemen," he said. "This is where we get out."

"Nuts!" exclaimed Link. "This isn't a jail. You have to take us to jail and book us."

Johnny Kerrigan leaned in at the door, hefting his heavy revolver in that great paw of his. "Do you go upstairs on your own steam," he asked softly, "or do I tap you on the skull and carry you up?"

Kovey and Link looked at him a moment, then at the gun.

"We'll go," said Kovey.

These were not the first guests of Mother Kelly's Green Room. On other occasions in the past, the Suicide Squad had entertained unwilling guests whom it was inconvenient to book. The very nature of the unconventional way in which they worked made it necessary to hold a prisoner incommunicado at times. Mother Kelly gladly aided and abetted them, though she knew that there was always a good chance of getting into trouble. But of one thing she was certain—that Kerrigan and Murdoch and Klaw never held anyone in that room who did not hugely deserve it.

Johnny and Steve came down after locking their prisoners

in, and joined Delameter and Dan Murdoch in the room next door to the one in which Abigail Dean and Nora Dixon were sleeping.

Dan was in a nasty mood. "I hear by the radio that you two lugs have been having yourselves a hot time."

He had the receiving set turned down low, and was picking up one of the all-night stations. *Three Little Fishes* was dribbling in on a record. Delameter was pacing up and down, nervously.

"There's going to be hell to pay in this town in the morning!" the old lawyer said. "Nicodemus Largo will have men out combing the city for us—"

"Not for you," Steve said, "or for me."

Delameter looked at him inquiringly.

Steve grinned. "He'll think we're both dead. He has no reason to believe that it wasn't the two of us who walked into that trap. And there's nobody to tell him otherwise. Kovey and Link certainly won't tell him."

"But he'll be looking for Kerrigan and Murdoch—and for little Nora."

THE THREE LITTLE FISHES came to an end, and the announcer said, "More news on that explosion at Twenty-fifth Street. Here's a bulletin issued by the Police Commissioner on the spot. It is now believed that the explosion was caused by the detonation of some dynamite that was stored there by the Largo Construction Company. The Company used the cellar of the abandoned building as a storage dump for explosives used in their building operations on the river front. The building itself is part of the old Horace Dixon estate, which is administered by Nicodemus Largo, president of the Largo Construction Company. Mr. Largo, who was notified of the accident, has come to the scene. He believes that some tramps must have taken refuge from the cold in the basement, and inadvertently dropped a cigarette which started a fire. At least two men are known to have died in the explosion, but it is impossible to identify the remains. And now, my friends, I give you that popular ballad, *The Last of the Ice Men!*"

Dan turned off the radio. He looked reflectively at Steve and Johnny.

"Did you hear that?" he asked. "Nicodemus Largo is at Twenty-fifth Street."

"A lot of good *that* does us."

"A bullet in the head would do him a lot of good," Murdoch said softly. "But we can't even afford the luxury of shooting him—yet."

Mother Kelly stuck her head in the door. "Telephone," she said. "Washington calling. It's your Chief."

Steve Klaw sighed, and followed her downstairs to the phone.

"Good morning, sir," he said.

"Steve!" the Director said tensely. "Have you any news?"

"Nothing good yet, sir. I'm sorry to say we haven't got to first base."

"Is there any chance you'll be able to accomplish anything before noon?" the Chief asked anxiously.

"We'll try our damnedest, sir."

"I'm counting on you three, Steve. I've been up all night, talking to Congressmen. They've been calling me on the phone every fifteen minutes. They're frantic with worry. If you don't crack this before Congress convenes, there'll be a scandal that will split the nation wide open."

"I understand, sir. We'll do everything in our power."

"I don't like to say this," the Chief went on slowly, "but if everything else fails, you must use Nora Dixon as bait!"

He paused a moment, then added, "Understand, Steve, the suggestion does not come from me. I have two members of Congress here at my elbow. They insist on my giving you these instructions."

"All right, sir," Steve said dully.

"Call me as soon as you have something, even if it's the last minute. Use the private phone number of the Congressional cloak room. I'll be waiting there."

"Yes, sir."

Steve hung up, and returned upstairs. "All right, boys," he said to Dan and Johnny. "It's double or quits. We shoot the works."

CHAPTER 6
CUSTOMERS FOR CASKETS

THE LARGO CONSTRUCTION COMPANY had a two-story black marble-and-silver building on one of the side streets just west of the River. Alongside it was a large private parking lot. The lot also held a number of metal sheds for construction materials. The street in front of the building was busy, at nine in the morning, with cars coming and going. Trucks were pulling out of the lot, loaded with workmen for the various jobs along the river front. A huge derrick truck lumbered out, the crane thrusting its gaunt frame for a hundred feet out behind. The crane operator sat in his caboose, facing the rear.

Stephen Klaw, at the wheel of one of the two limousines they had captured last light, had to wait till the immense derrick got out of the way. Then he tooled the car over in front of the entrance of the building. He turned and looked somberly at Abigail Dean and at little Nora Dixon, who were crowded into the front seat with him.

"You both know what you have to do?" he asked.

Abigail Dean was sitting, tight-lipped, her hands wrapped around her big black purse. "Yes," she said. "I know what I have to do. And I don't like it. But—I'll do it!"

Steve nodded approvingly, and looked down at Nora Dixon. "What about you, child? Are you ready?"

Nora had a big doll on her lap. It was a beautiful doll, with dark hair just like Nora's, and big eyes that opened and closed and rolled around. The doll was dressed in a plaid coat just like Nora's, and a little plaid hat to match.

Nora looked up trustingly at Klaw, and smiled. "I know what I have to do, too, Uncle Steve. And I *like* it." Her eyes were shining excitedly. "It's just like story hooks—you know, where little girls and little boys get a chance to help the police. Don't worry about me, Uncle Steve. I'll do my stuff!"

Steve sighed. "This is not going to be fun. Nora. It's dangerous."

"I like it."

He patted her shoulder. "You're a brave girl, Nora. And you too, Abby! Come on, let's go."

They got out of the car and went into the Largo Construction Company Building. There was a switchboard just inside the entrance. Significantly, it was operated by a man. There were several men around the place, apparently doing nothing in particular. But they looked hard-bitten, and ready for anything.

At the switchboard, Steve said, "I want to see Mr. Nicodemus Largo."

The fellow at the board glanced at Abby and Nora, then looked up, scowling, at Steve. "What name?"

"Tell him it's Stephen Klaw."

The fellow jerked in his seat, and his eyes narrowed. He started to make a signal to one of the men lounging near by, but Steve said swiftly, "You can also tell him that I've brought Nora Dixon."

"Oh!" The operator subsided in his seat, but his eyes were narrow and watchful. He plugged in and rang, and then spoke softly into the mouthpiece. He looked up at once, and nodded to Klaw.

"Mr. Largo will see you right away. I'll have you shown to his office."

He signaled to the man standing near the switchboard.

"Kinney, take these people to Mr. Largo."

The man, Kinney, was chewing a big wad of tobacco. He switched the cud into his cheek and said, "Follow me."

THEY WENT after him, toward the rear of the building. Steve threw a quick glance behind, and saw that two more of the

157

men who had been lounging around the entrance were following them. At the rear of the building, Kinney started down a flight of stairs.

"Is Largo's office in the basement?" Steve asked.

Kinney scowled. "You wanted to see him, didn't you? Okay, don't ask any questions." The other two men continued to follow down the stairs after them.

At the foot of the stairs Kinney led the way along a narrow corridor, and stopped at the far end, in front of the door. There was a bell button alongside it. Kinney pressed the button, and a buzzer sounded. The door swung open.

Kinney stepped aside. "Go on in," he said.

Steve motioned Abby in, then took Nora by the hand and went in with her. Almost at once, the two men who had followed them crowded in after them. They had guns in their hands now. One of them pressed his weapon against Steve's spine.

"All right, sucker," he growled. "Stand still." Then, to his companion, "Frisk him, Pete."

Pete came around in front, went through Steve's pockets, and took his two automatics. Then he expertly made sure that Klaw had no other weapons on him.

"Okay, Jock."

"Get going," Jock ordered, poking Steve in the back.

Steve obeyed, not saying a word. They passed through an anteroom, and entered a large office.

"Ooh!" exclaimed Nora. "What a big place!"

Klaw's eyes swept around the room swiftly. It did not have a single window. But there were several air-conditioning ducts which brought fresh air in. At a desk opposite them sat Nicodemus Largo.

He was a bull-necked man with a square, hard jaw and a thin, long nose. His eyes were black and stabbing as he studied Steve.

"Keep him covered every minute that he's in here, Pete," he ordered. "This is the most dangerous of those three G-men. If he does anything suspicious, shoot quickly. And shoot to kill. He has some trick up his sleeve, or he wouldn't have come."

Steve smiled. "Afraid of one man, Largo? And right in your own back yard?"

Largo smiled wolfishly. "Not afraid, Klaw. Just careful." His glance swung to little Nora. "So! This is my little ward. Come here, Nora. I want to talk to you. I'm your guardian, you know."

Nora didn't budge from alongside Abigail Dean. "You're a bad man," she said. "I don't like you."

Nicodemus Largo chuckled. "I don't blame you, Nora. Not when you know what plans I have for you."

"I know them," Nora told him defiantly. "Uncle Steve told me that you intend to kill me—and make it look like an accident."

"Indeed?" Largo raised his eyebrows. "And yet you came here with him?"

"Yes. Because Uncle Steve said if we were quick and sharp, we might turn the tables on you."

"Ah, so!" Largo breathed. His gaze swiveled back to Klaw. "I was sure you had a trick up your sleeve. But we are going to make certain that you *don't* turn the tables."

He looked searchingly at Steve. "Will you tell me just why

you took the risk of coming here this way? Surely you don't take me for a fool."

"We came," Steve said, "because I want to find that shipment of rifles and prevent it from leaving the country. I'm sure those rifles are being loaded somewhere around here, otherwise you wouldn't be so anxious to get rid of Nora Dixon."

"What makes you think Nora Dixon has anything to do with rifles?" Largo asked noncommittally.

Steve smiled tightly. "You're using the Dixon property to store the stolen weapons. That's why you don't want the estate to pass out of your own control."

"Who suspects this beside yourself?"

"No one."

LARGO WAS silent a moment. Then, "I suppose you know you've signed your own death warrant by giving me that answer? And Nora Dixon's, and this woman's?"

"*Somebody* is going to die this morning," Steve said steadily. "I can't say who, yet."

Nicodemus Largo showed his teeth. "I can. You three."

"By accident?" Steve asked sardonically.

"By accident," Largo said, nodding. He reached behind him and pressed a button. A panel in the wall slid open, revealing a tunnel. He addressed himself to Pete and Jock. "Take them through the tunnel to the dock. Bash their skulls in, and put them in the car they came in. Then leave the car on the incline, and fix it so that twenty-ton derrick truck seems to go out of control. Let it roll down the incline and smash into the car. It'll flatten them like pancakes."

160

His lips twisted in a smile. "A beautiful accident, don't you think, Mr. Klaw?"

"Fairly ingenious," Steve approved.

Jock poked him in the back with his gun. "Get moving—"

"Before we go," Steve said, "would you mind telling me, Mr. Largo, just where those rifles are being loaded? And how they're leaving the country?"

A light flickered in Nicodemus Largo's eyes. "You'll never know!" he whispered.

"In that case," said Steve, "I fear I must call your attention to Miss Abigail Dean, here."

Largo frowned. "What do you mean?"

"Observe," said Steve, "that she is holding a black handbag. You will note that she has raised it in the air above her head."

Abby had raised her handbag high in the air, and she was holding it by two fingers, delicately. She was managing to smile, but rather weakly.

"You see," Steve explained to Largo, "your men neglected to search Miss Dean's handbag. But even if they had, they would not have suspected the innocent-looking compact she has in it. That compact, Mr. Largo, is a very ingenious little trinket. It's loaded with fourteen ounces of picric acid, and is equipped with a miniature detonator cap charged with fulminate of mercury. Being in the construction business, handling explosives as you do, you will easily understand what will happen if Miss Dean lets her handbag drop to the floor." He smiled genially at Nicodemus Largo.

Abigail Dean held the pose, with the bag in the air.

Jock and Pete were staring at her with wide, terror-filled eyes. Largo was watching her suspiciously.

"This wouldn't be a bluff, would it?" he asked softly. "I can scarcely believe that you'd be ready to blow all of us, including the girl and yourself to kingdom come!"

"If you think it's a bluff," Steve said, "order your men to take the bag away from her."

Largo turned his glance back to Abby. Jock and Pete continued to stare at her, spellbound.

Unnoticed, Nora lifted up the plaid coat of her big, beautiful doll, and took an automatic pistol out of a cunning little pocket which had been sewn inside. She swiftly handed the pistol to Stephen Klaw.

He snicked off the safety catch, thrust Nora behind him, and said, "So sorry, gentlemen!"

Pete and Jock swung around, pulling the triggers of their guns as they did so. The shots blasted against the eardrums of everyone in the room, reverberating in the tunnel beyond. But they had fired hastily. The shots ploughed into the floor.

Cold-eyed, tight-lipped, Stephen Klaw coolly fired his automatic twice. He shot deliberately, and with intent to kill. Jock and Pete went down, a bullet in the heart of each.

Steve swung from the hips, brought his automatic to bear on Nicodemus Largo who was clawing a gun out of the top drawer of his desk. The gun was almost out when Largo saw the muzzle of Steve's automatic staring at him. He grunted and let the revolver drop back into the drawer. Then he raised his hands.

"I'm not armed, Klaw," he said.

Stephen Klaw smiled tightly. "I'm not ready to kill you yet, Largo. I want to know where those rifles are being loaded."

Largo's face was impassive. "I don't know what you're talking about."

Steve stepped over to the door. There was a bolt on it, and he shot it home—in case any of the gunmen had heard the shots. Then he crossed swiftly to Largo's desk, and pointed the automatic at him.

"Get up!"

LARGO WAS sweating a little. But his sharp, piercing eyes showed no fear. This was no cheap crook, who was ready to own himself beaten at the first turn of fortune. Steve could see the wheels revolving in Largo's mind, could guess that the man was ready to take advantage of the first favorable opportunity that offered.

Largo got slowly to his feet. "Well?" he asked sardonically. "How do you think you're going to get out of here? The building is full of my men."

"I'm thinking of the tunnel," Steve said.

Largo laughed. "That's full of my men, too. Do you think they'll let you pass?"

"I think they will!"

Steve motioned to Abigail Dean and Nora. "Come on, girls. Out through this sliding door!"

The girl and the older woman passed through the opening, into the tunnel. Steve forced Largo to follow them.

"Just tell me one thing," Largo asked. "Did that woman really have an explosive charge in her bag? I'm interested. I want to know if I lost out on a bluff."

Steve grinned. "When you tell me about the rifles, I'll tell you about that!"

As they stepped out into the tunnel, Stephen Klaw barely repressed a gasp of amazement. This was no two-by-four affair. It was an immense tunnel with a vaulted roof almost thirty feet high. The flooring was of poured concrete, and wide enough for two cars to drive comfortably abreast. Overhead there were neon lighting units and air-conditioning vents. Far back, at the right it was possible to see where a ramp led upward, possibly to the inside of some garage or warehouse. And to the left, in the direction of the river, there was a wall across the entire width of the tunnel. Plate glass windows in that wall afforded a view beyond, but Steve could not see what was on the other side, because they were almost two hundred feet away. What he did see, though, was a half dozen huge trucks, with men swarming around them, busily unloading wooden cases, which were immediately carried through a double doorway in the wall by porters.

"The stolen rifles!" Steve exclaimed. Then his forehead wrinkled. "But where are they taking them? There's no ship in the river at that point. We investigated—"

Largo laughed. "If you're lucky, Klaw, you may find out. If you're unlucky, you'll never know."

"I'll make the luck!" Steve grunted.

Down from the ramp at the right, a small sedan came rolling, with a single man at the wheel. The sedan slowed up as it approached them. Steve put the automatic back in his pocket, and waited. As the sedan came closer, the face of the driver grew clearer. It was Homer Monk.

Monk pulled up alongside Nicodemus Largo. For the moment, he was too excited to notice Stephen Klaw, or the fact that Steve's pocket was poking out into the small of Largo's back.

Monk stuck his head out of the window and shouted, "Boss! Two of those G-men are outside, at the back of the building. They're just over this part of the tunnel. They seem to be waiting for someone. What—"

"They're waiting for me!" Stephen Klaw said, stepping around from behind Largo.

Monk recognized him then and uttered a shout. He reached under his coat for a gun. Steve waited till he got the gun up, and out over the window. Then he shot him through the forehead.

Behind him, Abigail Dean uttered a little frightened screech, and Nora Dixon gasped. She covered her face with her little hands, and swayed on her feet. The shock had been too much for the child. She fainted.

Steve caught her in his arms, at the same time yanking his automatic out and keeping Largo covered with it. The busily working men down at the river end of the tunnel had not even heard the shot, for Steve had fired through the cloth of his pocket, and that had muffled the report. In addition, there was some sort of mysterious metallic clanking going on beyond the wall, which served to drown out any other sounds.

FOR A moment, Steve held the unconscious little girl in his arms. Largo looked at him sardonically.

"Well, Mr. Klaw? What are you going to do now?"

Steve slung Nora over his left shoulder, leaving his right arm free.

"You'll have to excuse me, Mr. Largo, but this is absolutely necessary."

"What do you mean?"

"This!"

Steve stepped in and tapped him along the side of the temple with the barrel of his automatic.

He hit him just hard enough to drop him. Then he thrust the automatic out into Abigail Dean's hand.

"Hold this gun, Abby," he ordered. "If Largo comes to, or if anyone goes for you, you shoot it by pulling the trigger. This is the trigger—"

"I can shoot a gun!" she said. "But where are you going?"

"To take care of Nora first," he told her. He climbed up on the narrow ledge, straddling the railing, with Nora still over his shoulder. A couple of feet away there was an iron ladder leading up to an emergency manhole. He climbed to the top, balancing Nora on his shoulder, and thrust upward at the manhole. It gave, and he pushed it over to one side, then stuck his head out.

Almost at once, he spotted Kerrigan and Murdoch. As arranged previously, they had stationed themselves at the rear of the building, to be ready in case he needed them. They seemed to be getting more restless by the minute. They were looking over toward the building, and they didn't see Steve's head poking out of the manhole. About fifty feet behind them, at the edge of the parking lot, was their car, with Pierre Delameter in it. The old lawyer had insisted on coming along.

Steve raised his voice cautiously and called, *"Hey, mopes!"*

Kerrigan and Murdoch jumped. They turned around, seeking the source of his voice, looking mainly toward the building, and not down at their feet.

Steve grinned. "You're cold, mopes!"

Both Kerrigan and Murdoch spotted him at the same time now, and they came running over. Delameter also came over from the parked car. Steve handed up the unconscious body of Nora Dixon.

"Take her to the car, Delameter," he ordered. "And drive like hell out of here. There's going to be fireworks popping in a minute."

Delameter didn't stop to ask questions, or to argue. He gathered up the frail, limp figure, and ran back to the car with amazing speed for his years.

Kerrigan and Murdoch climbed down the ladder back into the tunnel after Stephen Klaw. They asked no questions either. And Klaw vouchsafed them no explanations, except for one bit: "This is the blow-off, boys! It's the rifles!"

At the bottom, Abigail Dean was standing tensely, with Steve's automatic pointed at the recumbent Nicodemus Largo. He was conscious, but still groggy.

The three G-men reached the bottom, and Steve strode over to take his gun from Abigail. At the same time he called over his shoulder, "They're loading the rifles over at the river end, mopes."

Just then, Largo pushed up to his knees. He had produced a small whistle from a vest pocket, and he stuck it to his lips. Steve jumped for him, but was too late. A shrill, piercing blast emanated from that whistle, which traveled up and down the length of that tunnel with the startling stridency of an air-raid siren.

The men loading the truck stopped working and stood as if they had been turned to stone. That whistle blast evidently meant danger, for almost at once a small force of armed men in strange uniforms appeared through the doorway in the wall. They wore sailor's uniforms, but not American. Each of those sailors had a small automatic rifle at his shoulder. An officer in the lead motioned toward where Kerrigan, Murdoch and Klaw were standing, and shouted a command in a foreign tongue. At once, the armed sailors raised their rifles and sighted. The volley from those weapons would sweep down the length of the tunnel, would mow down the Suicide Squad, as well as Abigail Dean. That it would also kill Nicodemus Largo did not seem to matter. Perhaps the commanding officer of those foreign sailors had not noticed his prone figure.

Kerrigan, Murdoch and Klaw faced those automatic rifles shoulder to shoulder, screening Abigail Dean with their bodies.

"Okay, boys," said Dan Murdoch. "This is it. See you in hell."

"See you in hell!" echoed Johnny Kerrigan and Stephen Klaw.

This was the way they had always expected to go out. This was the way they wanted it to be when it came—on their feet, with guns in their hands and fighting against great odds for a just cause. They faced their fate like soldiers and gentlemen, smiling and without regrets.

THE OFFICER was just about to give the command to fire, and the Suicide Squad was just about to begin shooting, when

Nicodemus Largo uttered a hoarse cry and sprang to his feet. He began to run, weaving wildly, toward the foreign sailors.

Their officer recognized Largo then, and held his order to fire. Johnny Kerrigan deliberately raised his gun and sighted for Largo's swiftly pistoning legs.

He fired once, twice. The shots reverberated in the tunnel, and Nicodemus Largo went sprawling head first, both his legs buckling at the knees.

Now, the enraged officer of the sailors uttered a high-pitched command to fire. At the same moment, Stephen Klaw felt some one twitching his sleeve from behind. Abigail Dean thrust her purse into his hand.

"My purse," she said.

That was all Stephen Klaw needed. His eyes glittered. He snatched the purse from her and ran forward a few feet, drawing his arm back.

"Scram, mopes!" he yelled over his shoulder.

The sailors held their fire for a split-second, staring in amazement at this seeming madman who was charging them with nothing but a woman's purse in his hand.

And in that split-second. Steve hurled the purse. He threw it as far as he could, putting every ounce of his power behind it. The purse sailed through the air, describing a wide parabola, and landed with a thud at the feet of the officer.

The thud was immediately drowned out by the ear-shattering explosion that followed. The bodies of the officer and of his sailors dissolved into a welter of flying limbs and bits of tattered uniform. The whole tunnel rocked as if a giant were delivering million-pound sledge-hammer blows at it. A great, jagged hole was torn in the outer wall, and water from the East River came cascading into the tunnel like a mighty torrent, sweeping everything before it.

At the same time, the wall at the end of the tunnel was demolished. For a single brief instant there was a glimpse of a long, dark cigar-shaped metallic hulk, with a conning tower above it, and other sailors running about on the platform in panic. Then the sweeping water blotted it from view along with everything else.

The flood came tearing toward Kerrigan, Murdoch and Klaw, at a pace which would certainly make it impossible for them to escape on foot.

Abby had fainted, and Murdoch had her in his arms. Even if it were possible for an unencumbered man to outrace that sweeping torrent, Murdoch could never have made it, burdened with Abigail. And Kerrigan and Klaw wouldn't have left him there alone.

It was Johnny Kerrigan who got in motion, almost without thinking. He wrenched open the door of the sedan, and yanked the body of Homer Monk out, letting him drop to the swiftly flooding floor. Then he was at the wheel.

Murdoch had already slung Abby into the rear. Now he and Klaw jumped on the running board, and Kerrigan gave as superb an exhibition of driving in reverse as had ever been seen. He backed that car up the tunnel at thirty miles an hour and hit the ramp on the bounce, only inches ahead of the cascading wall of water which pursued them.

That car tore up the ramp like a live juggernaut, and broke into the open air at the rear of the parking lot. Kerrigan let her roll for a hundred feet more, and then stopped.

For a moment, all three of them watched the water forcing its way up the ramp.

Johnny wiped his forehead. "Well, guys, I guess that wasn't the time." He grinned. "Maybe next time."

"Did I see right, down in that tunnel," Dan Murdoch asked, "or did my eyes deceive me? Was that a submarine?"

"It was," Stephen Klaw said somberly. "It was a submarine belonging to a Central American country. That's the way they smuggled the rifles out of New York—literally under our noses. Largo built that tunnel solely for the purpose of loading the rifles into the sub. That's why he didn't want any interference with his handling of the estate. This property all belongs to Nora Dixon."

Dan Murdoch climbed in back and took Abigail Dean's head on his shoulder.

"You know," he said reflectively, "Abby is a good sport. And she thinks fast, too. Handing you her purse was a stroke of genius. Let's adopt her."

"Well," Johnny Kerrigan said, grinning. "We'll buy her a drink, anyway!"

CPSIA information can be obtained
at www.ICGtesting.com
Printed in the USA
LVHW052106080422
715715LV00009B/706

9 781618 276520